I0571617

BONED
EVERY WHICH WAY

A Collection of Skeletal Literature
2020

Edited by
Nate Ragolia

SPACEBOY BOOKS

Denver, Colorado

Published in the United States by:

Spaceboy Books LLC
1627 Vine Street
Denver, CO 80206

www.readspaceboy.com

Content from BONED: bonedstories.wordpress.com

First printed April 2021

ISBN-13: 978-1-951393-07-6

Profits from sales of this book will benefit Brink Literacy Project - brinklit.org

With infinite thanks to each and every contributor, reader, and dreamer who made BONED a beautiful project.

TABLE OF CONTENTS

October

November

December

DAY RUINER
SHANNON PILIPETSKII

One interaction with you
And I am totally spent
Is this what I can look forward to
After a long, complicated day
You chomping on
My bones and sinew
Sucking the marrow
From any given moment
And leaving me as carrion
By the wayside?
Day ruiner, that's you!

Shannon Pilipetskii is a wife and mom of two little boys, living in New Jersey. She likes travel, exotic food, nonfiction, and rap music. Many nights are spent staying up late writing. Coffee is in hand as she explores a new adventure, into the published literary world.

THE ESSENCE OF THE GAME
KARLO SEVILLA

They dribble somebody's skull
up and down the hardcourt:

The prized bouncing orb –
shaven, scalped, effaced –
changes hands among men
of two contending teams.

They hustle for possession,
and anyone who holds it,
when open and free
of jealous guards,
shoots the dry-skinned sphere
into mouth of iron agape.

Fanatic spectators erupt into frenzy
with every swish
into their inner circle
(and subside to a hush
when it sinks
into the others').

The real gladiator
has long fallen, though,
decapitated skeleton
buried somewhere
unacknowledged.

But he remains in the arena,
and a thousand fans
bear witness to his head
dribbled on the hardcourt.

Karlo Sevilla writes from Quezon City, Philippines and is the author of two poetry collections: "Metro Manila Mammal" (Soma Publishing, 2018) and "You" (Origami Poems Project, 2017). He was a runner-up in Submittable's 2018 National Poetry Month poetry contest and one of his poems is nominated by Ariel Chart for the 2018 Best of the Net Anthology. His poems have appeared in Philippines Graphic, Radius, Eclectica, Anti-Heroin Chic, The Ramingo's Porch, and others. He currently studies for the Sertipika sa Panitikan at Malikhaing Pagsulat sa Filipino (Certificate in Literature and Creative Writing in Filipino) program of the Center for Creative Writing of the Polytechnic University of the Philippines.

DANTE'S WAY
(SUL PERCORSO DI DANTE)
RON SINGER

Until my "retirement" thirteen years ago, I enjoyed a successful career as an actuary. Concurrently, I enjoyed an avocation as an amateur Dante scholar, an avocation I have since had more time to indulge. In fact, I am a charter member of the Metropolitan Alighieri Dante Society (MADS).

Here are a few details from the life and work of the Master that are germane to my story. Dante commences his poetic journey of revenge and redemption in the throes of a mid-life crisis:

> Nel mezzo del cammin di nostra vita
> mi rirovai per una selva oscura (Inf. 1.1-2)

Or (in my own translation):

> In the midst of life's journey,
> I found myself lost in a dark wood.

By the time he began his masterwork, Divina Commedia, he was languishing in exile:

> Tu proverai sì come sa di sale
> lo pane altrui, e come è duro calle
> lo scendere e 'l salir per l'altrui scale. (Par. 17.55-60)

> As the proverb goes, how salty the bread
> in another man's house,

how steep the stairs!

The principle of revenge in Inferno, the first of the three books that comprise the Commedia, is called "contrapasso": i.e., the punishment mirrors the crime. Yet the actual punishments that are meted out are often harsher, or less harsh, than the sinners would appear to deserve, even by the standards of early 14th century Italy. In many cases, Dante's own loyalties, passions, and quirks richly dye the contrapassi, as do the sinners' motives, virtues and emotions.

Take the "outing" of his beloved teacher, Brunetto Latini, who languishes in the Seventh Circle, reserved for those who have sinned against nature. This particular judgment is tempered in several ways. Looking down from a ridge above the one on which Brunetto must endlessly walk and burn, the contrapasso for "cruising," the pupil expresses his respect:

Io non osava scender de la strada
per andar par di lui; ma 'l capo chino
tenea com'uom che reverente vada.

'Though I dared not leave the upper path
to walk the lower one with him, I kept
my head bowed, as one who walks in reverence. (Inf. 15.43-45)

After prophesying his visitor's future woes, the political feuds that will drive him into exile, Brunetto alludes vaguely to his own sin:

In somma sappi che tutti fur cherci
e literati grandi e di gran fama,
d'un peccato medesmo al mondo lerci. (Inf. 15.106-08)

In sum, note that they were all clergy
or renowned scholars, befouled on earth by a single sin.

Note, too, the implicit boastfulness of "renowned scholars."

Brunetto further mutes his transgressions by graphically dissociating them from those committed by other gay men, including a sinner in the employ of Dante's archenemy, the "servant of servants," Pope Boniface VIII:

...e vidervi
s'avessi avuto di tal tigna brama,
colui potei che dal servo de' service
fu transmutato d'Arno in Bacchiglione,
dove lascio li mal protesi nervi. (Inf. 15.110-14)

...And if you had shown
a hankering for such filth, you might have seen
the one transferred by that servant of servants
from the Arno to the Bacchiglione,
where his sin-stretched organ finally expired.

In somma, one might say, Inferno is the work of an angry man who, having lost his way in life, is groping for truth and justice. But, even so, it is the prevailing malice (e.g. the incidental jabs at Boniface and his minion) that has endeared the book to seven centuries of readers –myself, included. In my case, a further reason the book speaks to me may be that, like the poet, I seem to have lost my way, and taken solace in revenge, though closer to the end of life than to the middle.

As another aside that I hope will prove illuminating (we old men are garrulous!), let me recall Dostoevsky's Underground Man. Quoting from memory this time, and in my own loose translation, "I am a sick and spiteful man. I think my liver may be diseased." That's me, except for the liver. Mine is fine, which is more than can be said for some of my other body parts.

Who am I, then? By name, Paul Wolf, I am an octogenarian whose years in exile on the island of old age (increasingly populous, nowadays) are about to end. My life was not, of course, always so. As mentioned, I spent my working years as an actuary. My single employer for more than four decades was what is called a "super-cat" re-insurance company. Specifically, my job was to use stochastic calculus, a branch of mathematics, to calculate the odds and costs of likely natural disasters, and to help my masters determine the rates at which they could very profitably re-insure companies that sold primary insurance against these disasters.

Over all the years, and especially near the end, with the advent of severe climate change, there had certainly been no shortage of catastrophes. But, contrary to popular opinion, the most successful super-cat re-insurance companies make more money when catastrophes proliferate –if they have good actuaries, that is, not to mention large capital reserves, or, as a contemporary vulgarism puts it, "deep pockets" (which is, strictly speaking, a dental term. I know about those from personal experience. The treatment is excruciating.)

Speaking of "deep pockets," as a highly competent senior employee, I was amply rewarded. Over the years, I was able to amass savings which, invested wisely, of course, would have enabled me to live very comfortably in retirement. But, owing to a major setback, what I came to desire more than money was to make those who had offended me live very uncomfortably. Not as uncomfortably, perhaps, as Dante's souls in Hell, but very uncomfortably. Actually (or, if you a devotee' of paronomasia, or puns, actuarially), it was my own masters against whom my wrath was directed. Although I hope you will agree that I had good cause, and that the plans for my revenge were clever, there is a strong probability that these plans are about to come to an end that is... catastrophic.

The precipitating incident took place at 9:15 a.m. thirteen years, two months, and four days ago. This, coincidentally or not, is the same time of day that I now sit here at my keyboard. Without any notice, whatsoever, I was summoned to the Personnel Director's office.

I knew what was coming. First, my workload had been steadily increasing for sixty-three months, as my greedy employers relentlessly downsized my department. Until four months before my summons, two survivors, both of us very senior, had been doing the work previously done by five, then four, then three. Two months after that, my co-survivor, a highly competent woman about ten years younger than I (i.e. in her early 60's), also disappeared. The next morning, a bright young thing was already ensconced at her predecessor's desk, sharpening multitudinous virgin pencils. (We still used them, in our "game.") I was introduced to the new employee by the Office Manager, who directed me to "show this newbie the ropes."

"Newbie!" Yet another neologism! And never mind the nautical cliché! Don't you love what is happening to the mother tongue? (Or is it, by now, the "parental" tongue?) Not that I am a prescriptive grammarian, someone, that is, who still believes English should assume the ostrich position, but the current rate of change is ridiculous. If languages were motor vehicles, there would be a massive pile-up on the Highway of Discourse.

At any rate, for me, "showing the ropes" was, to mix the metaphor, the handwriting on the wall. My own meeting with the new Personnel Director took place six weeks later. This would be the first time I had met her ("Laid eyes on her" sounds faintly salacious.)

"Hello, Paul," said the smooth-faced, forty-something African-American, offering me a firm handshake. "I have good news and bad news for you today."

As usual, the company had covered its bases, or its backside: a female of color, no less, in middle management! As for her "good news and bad news," we used to call such phrases "see-saw clichés," other examples being "hale and hearty," and "fat and forty." Whether hale or hearty, the new P.D., though forty, was anything but fat. Au contraire, she looked very trim in her black "power" suit (most definitely not a "Black Power" suit!). Her empathic smile could have illuminated the Empire State building. Were her teeth capped, or did she have good dental genes?

To skip the bulk of our short conversation –a monologue, really, interspersed with a few grunts from me– the good news was that my parachute would be quite generous, about 18-karat. The bad news was obvious.

Less obvious was the contrapasso I devised. About a month after my "termination" (not starring Arnold Schwarzenegger), I began to set a plan in motion. I was surprised to discover how easy it would be to get even with those ingrates, my ex-employers.

(Not) to divulge trade secrets, but I realized the firing process had been uncharacteristically sloppy. Yes, they had made me sign some forms: a guarantee of non-disclosure of proprietary methods; abdication of the right to work for competitors (with a long list of rivals, plus "any others"); a pledge not to contact any of the firm's other employees, past or present; and so forth. As most people know, forms like these carry varying amounts of legal weight, from zero, to "not if you have a decent lawyer." The only one that counted, the stricture against contact with other employees, could have been demolished in court by a summer intern. But, as I already realized, if the scheme I was about to undertake misfired, I might need not a lawyer, but an undertaker.

Even more remiss, perhaps, was the company's failure to change the locks. To make a long story short (I know, this one is already 1,650 words, and counting), I decided to contact my two immediate predecessors on the chopping block. As Google informed me, both were still among the living, and for a small fee, I obtained their current home and e-mail addresses. Both of these good folks, I hoped, might well harbor simmering grudges against the firm.

Via text message, I suggested we get together at a café equidistant from our three domiciles, to discuss "a matter of mutual interest." Vagueness was best. Let them think I wanted to start a new business, or something. Neither did I add, "for old time's sake," which would have been patently disingenuous, since, as colleagues, we had always hunkered down in the rich data of our separate projects. Within a few minutes, affirmative replies were forthcoming.

The next morning, at 10:30 sharp, we were ensconced at a corner table of the café, with baked goods and beverages of choice (hot, since it was February) in front of us. After minimal pleasantries, I opened the proceedings with a pre-prepared grabber: "I don't know about you two, but the company doesn't seem to have bothered to cancel my access." Their startled expressions told me I already had them on the hook. Although neither had touched their food or drink, they were practically salivating with curiosity.

"This is how I know. At the end of my termination interview, the P.D. -a new one, possibly after your time- informed me that my password would be invalidated in one hour. It was true, I checked. But, the other day, for some reason, I decided to try an old password, which I had temporarily lost ten years ago. Apparently, they had neglected to cancel that one, since lo and behold, it still worked! Maybe, they had been careless because they assumed my big severance bonus would guarantee undying loyalty. Ha! And there's more."

By now, Roger Mott, a big, red-faced man who must have been approaching seventy, and who obviously loved his food, was frozen, open-mouthed, with his fork poised in midair, a piece of baba au rhum dangling precariously from a single tine.

"Of course, even if they had tried to take proper precautions, they would still have had security issues, things they couldn't have guarded against. You know, it's not like, when they canned us, they forced us to eat lotus blossoms, to make us forget how the statistical models worked. I mean, we were the ones who designed those models, and the ones who wielded them all those years to make the firm filthy rich! But look at it from their point of view. What were they supposed to do, trade in good models for new, inferior ones?" Estelle

Saperstein, the third person at the table, and my immediate predecessor on the chopping block, was a tall, thin woman in her early seventies, about my age. Estelle had been a magna cum laude with a double degree in Math and Physics from someplace good – Stanford, I think. As I paused for effect, she was apparently unaware that she was stirring her latte with her right index finger. Either the latte was no longer hot, or she was.

Still cautiously, I nattered on. "Any hypothetical former employee still in possession of an active password, and who knew how to work the models, could either alter data in ways that severely reduced the firm's profits or, if said person preferred, partake of their assets!" I suppressed an impulse to grin or to wink.

"But that password, Mr. Wolf," objected hardheaded Estelle, "must only be operative in the company's internal network. Your putative hacker would need access to the office computers. Didn't they ask you to return your keys? Or do you have old keys, too?" When a serious woman like Estelle makes a lame joke like that, you can tell she is in the throes of some overwhelming passion –in this case, revenge and/or greed. I knew she was on board.

"Call me 'Paul,' please, Estelle. The old password works in my apartment, on my personal laptop."

"Wow, a live p-word!" cried Roger Mott, flipping the piece of baba home. "I never even thought of trying mine."

"Why should you have, Roger?" I replied. "An honest, loyal fellow like yourself? And I bet you're so honest," I said to Estelle, "that you never thought of trying yours, either. Besides, it doesn't matter whether your passwords work. Mine does." Estelle's finger had stopped stirring her latte, but it was still extended, as if she were checking the wind.

"Which caper should it be?" asked Roger, devouring the rest of his pastry in two huge bites. "Rob them blind, or make the business crash?" He was obviously a zealot.

"Why does it have to be either-or?" asked Estelle mildly.

"O, ho! You took the words right out of my mouth," I said, which was true. "But let's drink up, before our beverages get cold."

"May I propose a toast?" suggested Estelle, who now wore a loopy, myopic grin. "To larceny."

"To grand larceny!" cried Roger.

We drank to that, and agreed to meet again, two days later, same time, same place, which Roger dubbed "the war room." Meanwhile, I would set in motion the process of extracting company data. After I had paid the check, tip included, we shook hands and went our separate ways.

Let me underline the fact that, at each stage of my pitch, I had kept a weather eye out. If either of my co-terminate-ees had shown the faintest signs of panic or moral umbrage, I would have shut my pie hole fast, except for eating the apple pie I had ordered, which turned out to contain too much cinnamon, anyway.

In the event, I should have shut my P.H. Thirteen years later, this is no longer an option. So what! In for a dollar, in for ... damnation! But that, as a witty college professor of mine once quipped, is "putting Descartes before Ho-race" (which he pronounced with a French accent, making it sound like "horse").

I proceeded in logical order. To oversimplify, I would hardly have waited to rob the company until I had bankrupted them. Without getting too technical (since I assume the reader is not using this story as a sleeping pill), here are a few salient details. I should point out, in passing, that by the time the three of us reconvened, my larcenous maneuvers were already well under way. When I laid out the plan, far from demurring, Roger and Estelle seemed mesmerized.

Fleecing the Firm: Using pseudonyms, and what are called "margin accounts" (which basically means buying things with other people's money), in the course of a few months, with credits from several brokerage houses, I made about 100 separate purchases of company stock, each between 50 and 300 shares. I then sold all the shares at their current price (high). A few months later, after I had caused the stock to plummet [see infra], I re-paid the brokers in re-purchased shares (low).

Need I add that these machinations involved unnumbered Swiss accounts? All told, I probably netted about 57.36 million dollars. "Probably"? "About"? These qualifications stem from the fact that the purloined amounts are stated in 2005-dollar values. Of course, being a man of my word, my own share was a paltry 19-plus.

The larceny entailed one further wrinkle. I transferred our profits to the banks through a tortuous trail of fictitious entities, so that anyone who smelled a rat would have had to bait the trap and chase the rodent for months, through places to which the chaser could not have gained access. If that sounds murky, it was. The best way to understand it is to think of money laundering, the sort of thing you have undoubtedly read about in connection with spy rings and drug cartels.

Timing, as I said, was crucial. Immediately after my final purchase, I began the demolition phase.

Deep-Sixing the Corporate Vessel: This phase was also carried out by means of a single process, which involved something called "float." A bit more arcane than margin accounts, float is money set aside to meet anticipated claims. Normally (and don't forget, Roger, Estelle, and I wrote the book), the firm would invest according to the size of estimated future claims, and their time frame: the shorter the time frame (called "short-tail float," or STF), the more conservative the investments. My tactic now was to transfer a large percentage of the company's STF into dubious instruments, such as junk bonds and penny stocks. For long-term float, or LTF, I transferred funds from the current, more speculative instruments into high-quality, low-yield bonds, mostly ten-to-thirty year Treasury notes.

How, you ask, was I able to hide these manipulations from the company's current actuaries, not to mention its auditors? Dodging the latter, a highly competent bunch, was easy: I performed my statistical prestidigitations in the weeks right before the annual audit.

And let me tell you, that audit was a sight to behold! More than half of it was in BOLDFACE CAPS!

The way I fooled the actuaries falls under the heading, "so technical as to be soporific." (Caveat, lector! You can skip this paragraph.) As I just mentioned, my general strategy was to reverse the normal pattern of investments. The money transfers were made in the names of about thirty low-level company employees, and through a series of fictitious entities. By the time the actuaries could trace the paper trail, the damage had been done, apparently by the same people who cleaned their toilets and emptied their wastebaskets! A secondary pleasure was my knowledge that, when I was still with the Department, chicanery like this would have been detected almost immediately, and ruthlessly staunched.

Please note that the bear market in U.S. stocks did not begin until 2007, whereas my operations ended in mid-2006. In terms of the market collapse, I was a minnow, although, regrettably, the minnow's revenge occasioned extensive collateral damage, such as the bankruptcy of several insurance companies, with the concomitant loss of thousands of jobs. To make my omelet, yes, I broke a lot of innocent eggs. For that, I am truly sorry, but those eggs will be happy to learn that I am about to undergo a severe, if belated, punishment.

It is time to explain the hints I have been dropping like breadcrumbs about the demise of my scheme. About three or four weeks ago, one of my co-conspirators defected. And this, thirteen years after having gratefully acknowledged the receipt of some nineteen million dollars! In true cowardly fashion, she (yes, Estelle) confessed her defection via text message. By resorting to this, the most impersonal and pusillanimous mode of communication, she avoided facing my wrath, face-to-face:

Estelle: hi p. scnd thghts 2 rsky cnt me out. srry e

For the text-illiterate: "Hi, Paul. Second thoughts. Too risky, count me out. Sorry, Estelle."

"Too risky?" After thirteen years? To which circle of hell should such a disingenuous coward and ingrate be consigned? Too angry to argue, or even to reply, I realized I had a huge problem. Why had I ever thought I needed partners? I hate to admit it, but the reason may have been as simple as an old, newly unemployed man's loneliness. Well, soon enough, I would have plenty of company –kindred souls, too.

I mulled my options:

1. Murder the woman in some cruel, Dantean fashion. Not me! Grand Larceny is one thing, but... I wonder if, aside from the heat of battle, Dante ever murdered anyone.
2. Try to buy her silence with an additional tranche from my ill-gotten gains. As I said, my principal motive had been revenge, not greed.

But before I could decide to bribe Estelle, another shoe –the second? third?– fell. A few days after her perfidious text message, a registered letter arrived from the New York State Attorney General's Office, summoning me to appear before the Department of Financial Services, Insurance Division, at such-and-such an hour, such-and-such a date, in six weeks' time. Although the letter outlined a complex process by which I could request a postponement, what would have been the point? Conceivably, of course, the summons could have been triggered by something I had done while I was at the firm. Sure! It could also have been sent by hackers from Mars.

Yesterday morning, I saw something that made it certain the summons was, indeed, related to my 2005 peculations. A small death notice in the Paper of Record told me that Estelle Saperstein had passed, at the age of 83 (a widow, without progeny). So much for bribing (or murdering) this woman! Presumably, her long-harbored remorse had led to an eleventh-hour decision to spill the beans, including chapter-and-verse of the M.O. I had outlined to her and

Roger Mott at the café that fatal morning. Estelle had made a deathbed confession of my crimes.

A quick calculation told me that only two realistic options remained, federal prison or Dante.

Option One: I could spend my remaining days making license plates for twelve cents an hour.

Option Two: I could spend forever being torn limb from limb in the Second Ring of Circle Seven, the Violent Against Themselves.

This particular contrapasso is even more convoluted than most. As Dante learns from one of the damned, when a suicide's soul flees his despised body, the body is flung into a wood, where it metamorphoses into a thicket, the leaves of which the Harpies eat, inflicting excruciating pain. Since the thicket is a perennial, of sorts, the torture is unending.

After Judgment Day, when the soul descends to re-claim its body, an even more exquisite wrinkle kicks in. (I know, I know, a mixed metaphor.)

...ma non pero ch'alcuna sen rivesta,
che non e giuasto aver cio ch'om si toglie.
Que le straschinermo, e per la mesta
selva seranno I nostril corpi appesi,
ciascuno al prun de l'ombra sua molesta. (Inf. 13.104-08)

...But it would be unjust were we again
to clad ourselves in the flesh looted from our own souls.
So here we shall drag it, and in this gloomy wood
will our bodies hang, each one
on the thorn bush of its painful soul.

Caro lettore [Dear Reader], which punishment would you have chosen? Prison, I assume. But, as always, I am more curious than prudent. So I will end this long account by noting that I am about to proceed to the bathroom, where, among my panoply of medicaments is a paracetamol compound reserved for just such an eventuality as this.

Don't be shocked! Keep in mind that, were I to expire from natural causes in prison, I might meet the even more unspeakable fate of being consigned to the Ninth, and lowest, Circle, near the very bottom of which suffer those who betray their masters. But let's not go there!

Sources: All Dante quotations are from The Inferno, Purgatorio or Paradiso (transl. Robert & Jean Hollander, Random House, Anchor Books, 2000, 2004, 2008). The author wishes to point out that his narrator provides his own translations, sometimes also deviating from the critical commentary of the Hollanders.

Technical details about re-insurance:
   http://alephblog.com/2014/07/23/understanding-insurance-float/
   https://www.investopedia.com/university/shortselling/
   shortselling1.asp
   Berkshire-Hathaway Annual Report, 2017:
   www.berkshirehathaway.com/2017ar/2017ar.pdf

Please note that the company in this story is fictional, in no way modeled on either Berkshire-Hathaway's reinsurance division, or any other actual entity.

"Dante's Way" also appears in Ron Singer's *Gravy* (Unsolicited Press, July 2020), a multi-genre book about aging.

Stories by Ron Singer have appeared in many publications., He is also the author of thirteen books, including Uhuru Revisited: Interviews with African Pro-Democracy Leaders (2015),which is available in about 100 libraries across the U.S., and beyond. For details, please visit www.ronsinger.net.

OLD MEN WALK FUNNY (V2) / JUST BECAUSE, BAD HEART / CANADIAN SEASONS EXILED POET / INJURED SHADOW (V3)
MICHAEL LEE JOHNSON

OLD MEN WALK FUNNY (V2)

Old men walk funny with shadows and time eating at their heels.
Pediatric walkers, prostate exams, bend over, then most die.
They grow poor, leave their grocery list at home,
and forget their social security checks bank account numbers,
dwell on whether they wear dentures, uppers or lowers;
did they put their underwear on?
They can't remember where they put down their glasses,
did they drop them on memory lane U.S. Route 66?
Was it watermelon wine or drive in movies they forgot their virginity in?
Hammered late evenings alone bottle up Mogen David wine madness
mixed with diet 7-Up, all moving parts squeak and crack in unison.
At night, they scream in silent dreams no one else hears,
they are flapping jaws sexual exchange with monarch butterfly wings.
Old men walk funny to the barbershop with gray hair, no hair;
sagging pants to physical therapy.
They pray for sunflowers above their graves,
a plot that bears their name with a poem.
They purchase their burial plots, pennies in a jar for years,

beggar's price for a deceased wife.
Proverb: in this end, everything that was long at one time is now passive,
or cut short. Ignore us old moonshiners, or poets that walk funny,
"they aren't hurting anyone anymore."

JUST BECAUSE, BAD HEART

Just because I am old
do not tumble me dry.
Toss me away with those unused
Wheat pennies, Buffalo nickels, and Mercury dimes
in those pickle jars in the basement.
Do not bleach my dark memories
Salvation Army my clothes
to the poor because I died.
Do not retire me leave me a factory pension
in dust to history alone.
Save my unfinished poems refuse to toss them
into the unpolished alleyways of exile rusty trash barrows
just outside my window, just because I am old.
Do not create more spare images, adverbs
or adjectives than you need to bury me with.
Do not stand over my grave, weep,
pouring a bottle of Old Crow
bourbon whiskey without asking permission
if it can go through your kidney's first.
When under stone sod I shall rise and go out
in my soft slippers in cold rain
dread no danger, pick yellow daffodils,
learn to spit up echoes of words

bow fiddle me up a northern Spring storm.
Do you bad heart, see in pine box of wood,
just because I got old.

CANADIAN SEASONS
EXILED POET

Walking across the seasons in exile
in worn out house slippers, summer in Alberta prairies-
snowshoes, cross-country skiing winter in Edmonton, Alberta.
I'm man captured in Canadian wilderness, North Saskatchewan River.
I embrace winters of this north call them mercy killers.
Exiled now 10 years here I turn rain into thunder,
days into loneliness, recuperate loss relationships into memories.
I'm warrior of the trade of isolation, crucifier of seasons
hang torment on their limbs.
Ever changing words shifting pain to palette fall colors and art.
I'm tiring of Gestalt therapy, being In and Out the Garbage Pail.
I'm no longer an Aristotelian philosopher seeking catharsis.
My Jesus is in a vodka bottle soaked with lime, lemon juice and disco
dancing.
Pardon amnesty I'm heading south beneath border back to USA-
to revise the old poems and the new, create the last anthology,
open then close the last chapter,
collected works before the big black box.
I'm no longer peripatetic, seasons past.

INJURED SHADOW (V3)

In nakedness of life moves
this male shadow worn out dark clothes,
ill fitted in distress, holes in his socks, stretches,
shows up in your small neighborhood,
embarrassed,
walks pastime naked with a limb
in open landscape space-
damn those worn out black stockings.
He bends down prays for dawn, bright sun.

Michael Lee Johnson lived ten years in Canada during the Vietnam era and is a dual citizen of the United States and Canada. Today he is a poet, freelance writer, amateur photographer, and small business owner in Itasca, Illinois. Mr. Johnson published in more than 1037 publications, his poems have appeared in 37 countries, he edits, publishes 10 different poetry sites. Michael Lee Johnson, Itasca, IL, nominated for 2 Pushcart Prize awards for poetry 2015/1 Best of the Net 2016/and 2 Best of the Net 2017. He also has 168 poetry videos on YouTube: https://www.youtube.com/user/poetrymanusa/videos. He is the editor-in-chief of the anthology, Moonlight Dreamers of Yellow Haze: http://www.amazon.com/dp/1530456762 and editor-in-chief of a second poetry anthology, Dandelion in a Vase of Roses which is available here:https://www.amazon.com/dp/1545352089. Michael is also editor-in-chief of Warriors with Wings: the Best in Contemporary Poetry, a smaller anthology available now:http://www.amazon.com/dp/1722130717.

THREE MEALS A DAY
I.V. OLOKITA

Now she's laughing.

And for a moment she remembers how Daddy told her once that you cannot eat food when it's cold.

"But why, Daddy?" she asked him with her cute hazel and honey eyes she had when she was little.

"Because it's very comfortable for the flies, to sit on cold food," he replied and kissed her head with a fatherly tenderness and with his caressing voice he added that "flies simply spoil the taste of the food."

But Dina wasn't really interested in the food's taste or its temperature. All she wanted was for him to keep going, for him to sit a little longer by her side while she eats and tell her more of the nonsense he'd always share. And she didn't care if she had to eat the food when it was zillion degrees hot, or that her mouth would melt or that the flies will give the food a taste of wings and wind, as he once explained to her that flies do. The most important thing is that Daddy would stay by her for just a little longer. Only this one time.

But he did not. And Dina was angry. She just sat there and waited for the food to get cold and for the flies to come.

"Dina, your food will get cold," Daddy grumbled when passing by her on his way to stir the food inside the pot on the stove.

"I'm not eating until you tell me another story," said Dina with a cute little angry girl's voice.

"But sweetie," Daddy tried to explain, "Daddy has no time for stories now."

It was useless. She heard that story a million times before since Mom had gone to Heaven.

And he knew every time that this comparison was about to come, so there will be no choice, and he'll need to stop the whole world for her.

"You know, sweetie," Daddy gave up, lowered the gas under the pot and sat down next to Dina. "Both children and grown-ups have to eat to grow."

"Or they'll go to heaven like Mommy?"

"Yes," Daddy said. "Every child needs to eat and to drink. At least three times a day. Or else..."

"Or else he'd die," Dina completed his sentence, using a grown-up language and immediately added a curious question, "Daddy... God also needs to eat and to drink?"

"Of course."

"And who cooks for him and makes sure that he eats three times a day?" Dina added another question with a fearful voice.

"Ahhhh, don't you worry, sweetie," Daddy replied with a laugh and caressed her tiny face. "Because Daddy has a secret."

"A secret?" She asked in a whisper.

"A secret," Daddy replied and pressed his face to her ear to whisper. "But don't tell anyone. You promise?"

"I promise," Dina replied and turned her tiny lips to his cheek for a kiss.

"A week ago I tied God with a short blue thread to the fence behind the house and up to the white cloud," said Daddy in a whisper. "And at least three times a day I go out and pull down the thread without anyone noticing. And at first, God clings to the thread and doesn't want to get down. But afterward he gives in, and I pull the thread more and more until it reaches the ground and stops hovering. Then he sits down quietly by the table at the garden. I pour him hot-hot food so no flies would come. And he eats."

"Really, Daddy?" Dina asked, amazed.

"Really," Daddy said and laughed.

And now she cries.

23

For a moment she remembers that a few days later, Daddy disappeared on her as well.

And everybody said that he went to Heaven as well. And how miserable she was.

And Dina thought that it's not right that Daddy is not here by her said. She was angry with him for not telling her funny stories anymore, about food and flies. She ate all the hot food her aunt put on her plate, even though it wasn't tasty to her.

And for a moment, she would smile and turn to talk to the cloud.

"And who didn't eat?" she asks quietly, and the thread is still tied to the fence.

I. V. Olokita has been facing life-threatening situations most of his life, specializing in the management of medical aid to disaster areas all over the world. He has a BA degree in logistics, and an MPH degree emergency and disaster situations management. He also volunteers to rescue missions in disaster areas all over the world.

Olokita's first book (in Hebrew), Ten Simple Rules, was published in 2014. It won an Israeli literary prize and immediately made an online bestseller. The following year, another book by Olokita, Reasons to Kill God, made a local bestseller in Israel. In May 2016, his third novel, Wicked Girl, was published, to make another great success, and soon presents in English.

I. V. Olokita is a happily married father of two adolescents and a foster father of five cats and two dogs, and hardly ever sleeps. Instead, he spends his nights on writing. Olokita's books are characterized by direct writing, Turns wiry and witty, requiring the reader to delve into and maintain vigilance from the beginning of the book to its surprising end.

THREE FACES FROM WINTER
JOAN MCNERNEY

CHEAPSKATE

Grinding yellow teeth
this awful miser spits
out bleak afternoons.

With gnarled fists, he
collects freezing rain
to bury beneath snow.

THE 'LADY'

Prissy faced prude puts a
wet blanket over our plans.

Lowering frozen eyes,
she knots cold crystals
into braids of frost.

THUG

That tough guy...as mean as sin
and twice as slick...hunches his
shoulders stealing the sunshine.

Showing us who's in charge...he'll
make an offer we can't refuse
or crack a few bones over ice.

Joan McNerney's poetry has been included in numerous literary zines such as Moonlight Dreamers of Yellow Haze, Seven Circle Press, Dinner with the Muse, Blueline, Halcyon Days and included in Bright Hills Press, Kind of A Hurricane Press and Poppy Road Review anthologies. She has been nominated four times for Best of the Net.

ISIS, THE GODDESS
ALEXIS IVY

I used to be a girl full of holes. Everything used
to fall through. I have fallen to pieces. I collect
bones—instead of burying them. I see bones as a way

of recognizing a death not recognized. Bones are
something in myself I want the bones in myself
to give me a toughness. Bones are the skeleton

in my closet, the down to the heart
of the matter, the insides, the remnants,
on the way to the treasure. In the myth, Isis

gathered up the pieces of her twin brother.
She searched Egypt.   That is allegiance. I love
her for that, believe in her for that. She

never did find all the pieces. A fish swallowed
one in the canal. One of his ribs. In the end
she could not recreate Osiris. This is how

I learned that bones were to own, to rearrange,
save. Make a life more memorable. Tell the stories
I want to tell, change those stories. I go to places

I won't forget. Pick up the pieces of myself like Isis
picking up parts of herself. Never able to recreate.
And who would want to? A past like that?

———

Alexis Ivy is a 2018 recipient of the Massachusetts Cultural Council Fellowship in Poetry. Her first poetry collection, Romance with Small-Time Crooks was published in 2013 by BlazeVOX [book]. Her second collection, Taking the Homeless Census won the 2018 Editors Prize at Saturnalia Books and is forthcoming in 2020. She is a Street Outreach Advocate working with the homeless and lives in her hometown, Boston.

BEYOND, BELOVED
CHRISTOPHER BLAKE PINGLETON

I struggle, climbing the stairs
as I make my late night climb.
I balance another basket of my late night findings,
up the stairs in my lonely home.
I dare not trip and fall,
or else all that I have gathered will go to waste.

One step here, one step there.
I carefully make the turn,
and gently place my basket on the ground.
There, now I pull the cable, and release the attic stairs.
Lift, lift, lift,
Carefully, I climb another set of stairs.

It's dark, much too dark to keep going.
Again, I place my basket down with the utmost care.
Pulling out a lighter, I flick, flick, flick.
One, two, three, nine candles later.
My altar is now alight, and now,
I can continue my work.

My basket, I've kept closed and close to my chest,
I now open up.
Dirt, decay, wood, and mementos.
Finger bones, bottled up feelings, and locks of hair.
I begin work on my beloved altar.
Many months gone by, but with patience, it's nearly complete.

A dash of powdered grave dust, sprinkled across the altar.
A mixture of her blood, and my tears, I paint on this altar.
Her bones, I align, adorn, and decorate this beloved altar.

At the heart of this beloved altar,
sits the skull of my beloved,
surrounded by bones made of her former life.
Her spine, ribcage, and all.
It is... a vision of true beauty, an otherworldly sight.

But suddenly, the window of my attic bursts open,
a vicious wind slithers through my attic
and my beloved shrine!
I try to protect it, but the wind refuses me!
The candles are snuffed by this heartless gust.

I rise, but am halted by an unknown force.
Has my beloved come to me, at last?!
But oh, her grip is strong, so forceful!
Her once delicate hands, now sharp and wretched,
they squeeze my throat.

Something comes to my ear,
a cold, raspy, wrathful voice,
with the tone of an angel!
She says to me, with utmost hatred,
"I hope you're happy with yourself."
With a crushing force on my throat, I'm thrown to the floor.

Oh, how she stands!
Oh, how she glares!
Even in her state of hellish rage,

she is truly a work of art,
even after death!
Her bones, her rotten flesh, and her coal, black eyes!

She takes a step... and then another....
I begin to cry, happily,
as my beloved begins to crush my neck with her decayed feet!
I begin to shudder with delight,
as my vision begins to fade.
Her burning, reddening eyes
see me off, into the afterlife.

I'll see you again, my beloved!

I swear it.

Christopher Blake Pingleton, born and raised in a quiet part of Oklahoma, is a newly established writer in Oklahoma, having graduated from Tulsa Community College. He still lives in the quiet area of Oklahoma, dreaming of new ways to bring his thoughts to life.

AFTER THE STORM
CHRISTINA PETRIDES

Skeletons of skinned umbrellas
Snatched and eaten midflight
Litter the sidewalk
With leaves and branches
Rags snarl the corners
Of stepping stones
A torrent of white water
Tumbles down the spillway
Scores of sea roaches
Frisk about the sunny beach
Dark clouds throw themselves
At the northward mountain

Christina E. Petrides is an expatriate American living on a small Pacific island where all the magpies and the palm trees are imported, but the rice wine is indigenous and delicious

SHARD
SALVATORE DIFALCO

My wife Karen and I caught a redeye from Toronto to San Francisco for her brother Graham's memorial service. He'd died the week before after a two-year battle with colon cancer, and had been cremated. Shortly before he passed, he made it known that he wanted his ashes scattered near the Golden Gate Bridge, on a strip of beach where, before getting ill, he liked sitting zazen.

That morning we were joined on the beach, in the shadow of the Golden Gate Bridge, by my mother-in-law Marilyn, Graham's ex-wives Lily and Brenda, his daughters Chloe and Izzy, and his son Willy. Sunny but windy, the Golden Gate Bridge looked sinister against the sharp blue skies. Nearby Alcatraz loomed in high definition, ever ominous, surrounded by white-spiked waters. Maybe lack of sleep explained it, but the entire morning felt off.

Teary-eyed and morose, we huddled near the water. My mother-in-law, holding a brass urn, said a few words but I could hear nothing on account of the wind. When she finished speaking she uncapped the urn, turned it upside down and shook it violently. Amid the swirling ashes, I watched a shard of bone drop out of the urn, not far from my mother-in-law's feet. Caught up in their grief and the maelstrom of ashes, no one else noticed. As everyone turned and hurried off to the vehicles, I snatched up the shard—about two inches long—and pocketed it.

I said nothing to Karen about it. I knew better. It would have either weirded her out or sparked a battle. That night, at the hotel, I examined the shard in the bathroom. Dark-edged and dry as chalk, I had no idea which part of Graham it represented. Could have been a piece of leg bone, the femur perhaps, or part of a rib. Seemed too thick to be skull. I sniffed it, then stashed it in my toiletry kit. The smell—of char and vaguely fecal—stayed with me when I finally went to bed.

"You okay?" my wife asked.

"Yeah. You?"

"I'm okay," she said. "Gammy's at peace now."

"Yeah," I said. "Goodnight, Karen."

"Night."

We touched lips and she turned her back to me. She hated sleeping face to face; not that my breath reeked, but the heat of it annoyed her.

A lot of things about me had started annoying her around the time Graham got sick. The way I dressed. How I ate. The way I walked. The way I sat. I couldn't do anything right and everything I said caused offense. And rather than softening her antipathy toward me, grief for her brother had sharpened her teeth and claws.

Unable to hush my brain, I lay there awake for a time, a million random thoughts bashing around like bumper cars. Karen had fallen asleep, her thin body motionless. She never moved a muscle when she slept, strangest thing. After an hour of accelerating cogitation, I got up in a sweat and went to the bathroom. I hit the light and started. I looked completely fucked up. I splashed cold water on my face, took a drink from the tap and toweled off. Then I unzipped my toiletry kit.

I had liked and respected Graham. He was a decent brother-in-law, and we'd shared a love of film noire and NFL football among other things. Before he moved to San Francisco he'd lived in Brooklyn for a time and I had enjoyed several stays with him, his second wife Lily and my nephew Willy in their brownstone apartment. But family conflicts arose that kept him aloof for a few years until he fell ill, and even then it took considerable coaxing from Karen for him to make peace with his parents.

I looked at the bone shard again. It struck me as something almost comical: holding a piece of my brother-in-law's bone in a hotel bathroom. A practising Buddhist, I wondered if he would have found some humour in all this. I wrapped the shard with tissue paper and put it back in the kit, intending to dispose of it before we left. I returned to bed and finally managed to fall asleep.

We spent two more days in San Francisco with the family. Tensions were high. The kids quarreled over things Graham had left for them. Izzy wanted his I-phone. Chloe would have none of it. Graham's ex-wives bickered over a book, Isaac Babel's Red Cavalry—a surprising contest. Marilyn broke everyone's balls. Karen and I barely talked on the last day, a drizzly affair that chilled the bones and tanked the spirits. I never thought San Francisco could be so cold.

The flight back to Toronto was delayed, apparently for a terrorist threat that twelve hours later was deemed a miscommunication. Finally Karen and I boarded our plane. We spent the flight in stony silence, her occasional glances barbed with contempt.

"Just say whatever the fuck is on your mind," I told her as quietly as I could.

"I hate you," she said, before storming off to the lavatory.

The words stung. I had no idea what prompted them. Maybe I was approaching our rift all wrong. A soft touch was needed. She said nothing when she returned.

After disembarking we headed to Canada Customs. When the officer asked if I had anything to declare I said I did not. I hadn't so much as purchased a keychain in San Francisco. Karen also had nothing to declare. The only memento of Graham she'd secured was a clay Buddha statuette. Nevertheless, when we went through the scanners, a latex-gloved officer asked me to open my leather carry-on.

The officer immediately plucked out my toiletry kit and unzipped it. He found the clump of tissue paper, unrolled it and held Graham's bone shard up to the fluorescent light.

"Sir," the officer said, holding the shard at arm's length, "what is this?"

I blinked hard. I didn't know what to say. Or rather, how could I be truthful?

Karen looked at me, not with anger, or any visible emotion except maybe pity, and at that moment I knew why she had grown to hate me.

Salvatore Difalco is the author of 4 books. His short fiction has appeared in many print and online formats. He splits his time between Toronto and Palermo, Sicily.

website: http://saldifalco.weebly.com

INFINITY
LILY TIERNEY

The blood no longer is present
as a skeleton's hand reaches for the past.

Life no longer is alive with choices
as bones recycle images and experiences
that once were.

A lost love pumps its heart
as bones crack one by one
to enter eternity.

The skeletal remains are consumed
rushing toward infinity.

Lily Tierney's work has appeared in The Stray Branch, Illumen Magazine, Harbinger Asylum, Veil: Journal of Darker Musings, *and* Jellyfish Whispers. *She enjoys writing poetry and flash fiction.*

MACAWS
STEVEN TRANSLATEUR

Dorothy Shiinic knitted from dawn to dusk, everyday passionately, not knowing what else to do. She was so reticent and fearful, she could hardly form a relationship with anybody other than her pets; and they were plentiful: snow ball the cat, Hemlun and Amlun the hamsters, Betty and Tethy and Pethy the angel fishes, Gara and Fara and Cara and Tara and Lara and Para and Mara and Jara and Dara and Rara and Yara and Kara and Zara the guppies, Gissy and Issy and Bissy and Nissy and Fissy and Jissy and Yissy the catfishes, and George the glaucous macaw! She pampered them and they loved her.

But she was still lonely.

She lived on a quiet block in the suburbs. Her next door neighbor liked cats also and had four bony felines: Autumn, Spring, Summer, and Winter! And they each had a hued tag with their name on it. Their owner was a fascinating comrade named Akuva Smethe, a distinguished and witty widow who had tea with Dorothy once a month and counted that as almost her only contact with anybody during the year.

"I want to find Mister Right while I can still conceive," lamented Dorothy to Akuva one day at their tea meeting.

"Try nightclubs or hobby places," suggested Akuva.

So she started her hunt at shopping centers and bowling alleys and the community park.   Sometimes she would strike up a conversation with somebody she thought was attractive.   These encounters were interesting but usually did not lead to anything more than a curt, "Have a nice day," after them.   She was getting desperate. Her loneliness was overwhelming.

Then she also began hanging out in pet stores, quietly, minding her own business, tracing the aisles and then finally making a small purchase after a few hours. She did this every day. And then one day, Lythe Brove, fireman, entered the establishment and sought the bird section.

"Excuse me," Dorothy uncharacteristically boldly declared, "but are you looking for tropical bird seed also? Such birds are so rare."

"Indeed," Lythe replied. Then he took a bag and was off. "Have a swell day, Madam," he said in parting.

She could not help notice that Lythe came in an off duty fire vehicle.

Hmmmm., she thought to herself. How can she get the attention of a gorgeous fireman?

Lucky for she, the pet store had a "Bring Your Pet" day. She brought George her macaw and Lythe Brove showed up with Lidia, his macaw. After seeing a presentation on bird care, Dorothy remarked to Lythe that his bird was looking somewhat emaciated or *** bony, and probably could use a different sort of feed. He agreed and asked what she does to keep George healthy.

She suggested buying a premium brand of feed. And so he did.

They both noticed that their birds seemed to have a fondness for each other. Dorothy hoped that her relationship with Lythe would become like that. Then they parted.

Then a month later, by coincidence. she had to call fire emergency; Autumn and Summer had climbed too high a branch on an elm tree. "Help," she said. "My neighbor's cats are stuck up a tree."

And the firemen came, including Mr. Brove. They used a cherry picker ladder to rescue the animals.

"You are Mr. Wonderful," declared Dorothy. "Please come by for dinner tonight and bring Lidia!"

And so he did. She cooked a feast of roast beef, mashed potato, brussels sprouts, vanilla ice cream, and pecan pie. During the dinner, they were both silent because of how shy they were.

Dorothy had grown up not speaking to nearly anybody. She was normally reticent. Her comrades had to force themselves into her life to get any response from her. Still, she had the right to be left alone. Though mental health professionals nearly labelled her as autistic. She skipped her prom because of her inability to say "yes" to the five people who had requested her presence. Lythe was the only one she had any real interest in communicating with at that time, but she found it hard to say anything because of her personality.

Lythe was equally reserved. He spoke to almost nobody except his pet macaw. Lythe and Dorothy were made for each other!

After supper, Dorothy showed Lythe her glaucous macaw George again. It still impressed he. Lidia and George starting making sounds and falling in love and this was an impetus for a relationship between Dorothy and Lythe. The pets were chatty, and this set an example. Soon Dorothy and Lythe were talking to each other and opening up.

She knitted Lythe an entire, magnificent sweater collection as an engagement gift. They were of all patterns including solid, paisley, stripes, trapezoidal, starred, rectangled, and checkered–and of all colors including red, orange, blue, green, indigo, and violet. They wowed Lythe who began wearing them immediately.

Two months later, Dorothy and Lythe married.

Now George and Lidia, the glaucous macaws, beautiful birds with blue plumage and gray heads and pleasant dispositions, have companions too!

Steven Translateur's work has appeared in a variety of publications including MEMES, MIND IN MOTION, and NEXT PHASE.

TASTES LiKE PEHHiES
JUSTiH FREDERiCKSEH

He was delicious. Luke Price had grown up to be quite the man; he stood six feet- three inches tall, had luxurious blonde curly hair, green eyes and had the body of a Spartan. He ran every day, like clockwork. At five-thirty, the lights in his bedroom came on and in ten minutes he would be off to run the neighborhood and into Piedmont Park. Luke would run at a pace that few could keep up with, especially for that amount of time and would return home at seven to get ready for class. From the outside, it looked as though he had a perfect life. He was going to Emory, had a bright future ahead of him, lived in a prestigious home and had never wanted for anything.

Luke had never wanted for anything, but for his parents to still be alive. They were on vacation in Nepal; his father was writing a book about the adventures of a child that walked from Tibet to India to escape genocide from China and he wanted to travel the route to get a true sense of the terrain. They were happy together, seeing the world and sharing experiences. On a road near Pokhara that ran alongside a mighty roaring river, the Price family discovered just how dangerous the trek was. At the base of the mountain that led into the village, the road met with the Seti Gandaki River. The road ran parallel to the rushing waters and was only protected by a couple of feet of embankment. The earth was saturated and their jeep swayed heavily as it tried to navigate the thick mud. The intensity was palpable between the group as they exchanged looks of alertness.

A tourist van was coming down the mountain and slid into their jeep, crashing them into the soft mud embankment. The mud gave way and the waters hurled them into its grip. The crash had instantly killed the driver and badly injured his mother. She was bleeding and was unconscious. The freezing waters filled the car as it ricocheted off giant boulders, lodging the jeep between two boulders and securing it from its violent journey downstream. Luke's father grabbed him and pushed him through the windshield onto the top of the boulder. Luke's tibia had broken the skin and was bleeding profusely. Just as Luke had begun to turn around on his belly to reach for his family, the river surged and engulfed the jeep, taking his parents with it. The mighty Seti Gandaki had claimed its victims, yet again.

Luke returned home a shell of a boy with no one he could turn to except, for Walt Shoeman, the neighbor two houses down. Luke didn't have any close friends his own age and found his high-school years to be hollow because the other students were shallow and boring to him. The students always thought he was stuck-up; he never went to their parties or hung out with them. Luke's life experiences made him mature and disconnected from his peers. He had traveled the world with his family on trips to strange lands and tried amazing foods that his mom was introducing him to so that she could bring the recipes back to her Midtown restaurant. His close relationships with adults were what excited him more than any party could. He had no other family to speak of and found himself inundated with lawyers and paperwork. He had to make decisions about the restaurant and his dad's manuscripts that Walt was kind enough to help explain and help him with. Luke had inherited millions from his parents' estates and his childhood home. He was the last of the Price family and became determined to carry on the reputable family name.

The neighborhood had changed so much over the years, but Luke had remained one of the few locals that were born and raised in town, keeping the heritage of Midtown alive. His parents had come from old money and purchased their four-story home in the heart of Midtown on 7th and Myrtle in the 80's. The neighbors were friendly and had lived among them for years. Two houses down lived Walt. Walt had lived in the neighborhood for years while he worked as a medical doctor for the Marines. His house was a single-story bungalow, one of the few small homes left on the street. Luke's dad was working on a project about the military and how the medical doctors see the worst of war. Walt was all too happy to share the details because he thought people should know the effects that war has on the human body and about the dedicated men and women who devote their lives to helping the soldiers heal. Luke's dad and Walt became friends, often having dinners in the spring on Walt's perfectly landscaped courtyard that overlooked his pool and his amazing garden with beautiful flowers everywhere. Luke always wondered why Walt's house was so small compared to theirs, but the landscape made up for the one story home.

Luke first discovered his attraction to men during the summer break before they went to Nepal. Luke had picked some herbs and vegetables from his garden that Walt had helped him build two summers before and wanted to bring them to Walt. Luke walked into the backyard through the rot-iron gate on the side of the house to see Mr. Shoeman sunbathing naked next to the pool. Luke crept quietly. He had often found men attractive but had never really seen a man like this before. Walt was older, but had the body of a hard-trained military man. His tanned skin glistened with sweat that streamed over the muscles and pooled at Walt's navel. Walt was erect and had begun pleasuring himself. Luke found himself at full attention himself and squeezed the bulge in his shorts. As Walt rolled his head he noticed Luke near the house. He didn't stop but gestured with his icy blue eyes for Luke to join him. Luke stripped and straddled Walt as they climaxed together. "Good boy," Walt grunted out. "I-uh..." Luke tried to mutter. "It's ok. It's perfectly natural. You're eighteen and a man. Men have needs. I wondered how long it would take you to realize..." "I brought you some veggies from the garden." "Thanks, Luke." Walt licked his lips as he watched Luke walk away. Luke quickly got dressed and left as quietly as he had entered. The thrill of what he had just discovered about himself had shaken him. He felt like a part of him that he hadn't acknowledged was set free. Walt set him free.

Luke found himself going over to Walt's house regularly and gave his virginity to a true specimen of a man, a brute, a warrior but who was gentle with Luke. His hands were soft but strong. They held him in a way that melted Luke into him. Those icy blue eyes looked into Luke's soul, they were connected. Walt was the only one Luke could turn to after the tragic accident. He was the only comfort Luke had. They spent many nights together, sharing stories about Luke's parents, cooking, working out, making love, watching movies and grew closer. Walt helped Luke organize the financials and guided him through school. Walt's world experience was intriguing and kept Luke asking questions. Walt meant everything to Luke. They were happy together, spending almost every day together for three years.

Luke started noticing that Walt would go quiet at times, sitting at the table, staring off into space. An expression of regret and hatred blanketed Walt, sending chills down Luke's spine. They talked about how Walt's last tour was different than any before. He wasn't working on the soldiers, but the prisoners that had undergone various forms of torture and Walt's job was to keep them alive during the interrogation process. The things he saw done to the human body cracked his psyche with remnants of that past starting to seep out.

The sex had always been amazing, but Walt grew more and more aggressive in his methods. His once passionate and tender love became fierce and painful. Walt was becoming more and more demanding of his sexual expectations. Their relationship became strained when Walt had introduced leather and bondage to Luke. At first it turned Luke on, the smell of leather and sweat, but the intensity in Walt's eyes retracted Luke from the pleasure. Walt had built a dungeon of sorts in his basement; chains hung from the wall with handcuffs, a leather sling hung from the ceiling and had a steel table with leather straps. Luke wanted to please Walt so he dressed the part and played along. Walt brought Luke to the brink between pleasure and pain. The sex became sessions of pain and tolerance that Luke found to be degrading. Walt whipped him with an intensity that turned from pleasure to fear. "Stop! Stop! I'm done!" Walt tightened the straps around Luke's wrists. "You're done when I tell you boy!" "Stop! Please! You're hurting me! Sir!" Luke had tears falling over his cheeks. Walt walked over and licked them. "Delicious." Walt loosened the straps and walked upstairs, leaving Luke in the dark basement. Walt got what he wanted that day, pain, real pain.

Luke didn't come back after that. Love had faded into fear and Luke avoided Walt for a week. Luke thought hard about whether he wanted to continue seeing Walt and realized that it was the end of the relationship. He called Walt to join him for dinner. "We need to talk." "Look, I didn't mean to..." "Can you just be here at seven?" "Sure. See you then." Luke prepared a meal fit for a king. Luke cleaned rack of lamb the way his mom taught him, prepared roasted vegetables from the garden and selected a vintage wine from the cellar; a bottle of Romanee-Conti DRC 1990 would be perfect. Luke's dad had bought it while on a trip to the U.K. at the Sotheby's London in 1996 for about twenty-eight thousand dollars and was saving it for their twentieth anniversary. Luke wanted the night to seem well-thought out and intended the break-up to go smoothly. This was hard for Luke, he didn't want to hurt the man that had been there for him through the worst part of his life, his first love, his 'Daddy'.

The doorbell rang. It was exactly seven. "Come in." "I brought dessert. Dark chocolate truffles. Your favorite." "Thank you. Wine?" "Sure." They sat at the dining room table with the spread of food between them on the dark mahogany table. "Looks amazing." "I wanted to talk..." "Look, I'm sorry about the other night. I got a little out of hand. It won't happen again." "Walt, you have been there for me through so much. I have loved you so much, but I need to be on my own now." Walt sat quietly. He didn't even blink. "You are a wonderful man, but I am not into the kind of things you are. You scared me. I told you to stop and you just kept going. That was the first time I was afraid of you." "I thought you liked it. I only wanted to keep you happy." Luke reached for Walt's smooth hands. Walt pulled them away and took a drink of the wine. "This wine is delicious. Vintage?" "It is." "This is it, huh? The end?" "I love you, Walt. I need to be on my own, though. I want us to stay friends. I thought this would be special and show you how important you are to me." "I see. I suppose this is goodbye."

Walt looked stoic. There were no tears, no pain, just emptiness. His eyes went black as he got up from the table and walked towards the door. "Walt, wait." Luke walked over to him. "Goodbye, Luke." Walt leaned in for one last kiss. Luke couldn't resist and leaned in. They embraced and kissed heavily, Walt groaned. "What the..." Walt bit Luke's tongue, drawing blood. Luke pushed him away. "Get out!" Walt stared at Luke with those icy blue eyes as the blood dripped down his chin, "Delicious." He walked out the door and into the night. Luke bolted the door and went to clean up his mouth. The wound would heal, but his love was broken.

Luke was finishing his junior year and started applying for grad school. He applied to only one school, Emory. His dad and mom went there and he wanted to honor their memory by continuing the tradition. He met with the board for his interview and was accepted almost immediately. He stood in the elevator, relieved and proud. "You got in?" a voice asked from behind him. "Wha- Sorry. I didn't see you there." "Didn't mean to scare you. Just noticed that you looked like it went well. I'm Logan." "Hello. Luke." The two men shook hands. "I just got in myself. Law School. What are you going for?" "Finance Strategy and Markets." "Ah. Sounds interesting. Maybe you could tell me about it over coffee?" "Uh- ok. Yea, sure." The men exchanged numbers and met for drinks.

Luke and Logan became quick friends. They spent their extra time running together and hanging out. Luke found comfort in their relationship, Logan was easy to get along with. Logan came from a small town in South-Georgia and had earned a full-ride to Emory for his outstanding scholastic achievements. Logan was everything Walt was not. He was short and thin with a gentle confidence; he wore these thick-framed glasses that almost looked like he was trying to be funny and thick black curly hair that he greased down. Logan was quiet, but funny, always telling awkward jokes that made Luke laugh to the point of tears. Logan filled the hole in Luke's life that had been missing, not a caretaker, not a role model, but a friend, an equal in life that made Luke feel safe around him. Logan was the one person who truly understood and accepted Luke as he was. They shared stories from their childhood and how they felt growing up different from the other kids. The two found themselves in a blossoming friendship.

Luke felt lonely in that house all alone, so he decided to offer for Logan to move in. "Logan, I was thinking that instead of you moving back home for the summer, you could move in here. I know we haven't known each other long, but thought that it would be nice to spend some more time together. You can have any room you want; besides, you are already here almost every day anyway." "Uh- I'm not so sure, I don't have that kind of money to..." "No worries. You would be doing me a favor." "Ok. Sure. Could be fun. I would have missed all those amazing dinners you cook." "Great! It's settled then."

Logan moved in the day after finals. Luke had just grabbed a box and went inside when Walt walked up to Logan's car. "What are you doing here?" "Excuse me? Who..." "Never mind who I am. What are you doing here? He's mine. You don't belong here." "I'm not sure what you are talking about. Are you and Luke..." "You have been warned." And just like that, Walt walked away. Logan was just standing there when Luke came outside. "Why are you just standing there?" "I think I just met your ex?" "What? He knows... Was he tall with big muscles? A leather daddy type?" "Yes! He scared the shit out of me! He said I was warned." "I'm sorry. That was Walt." "Oh, that was him?" "Yes. Just steer clear of him." "Are you sure this is a good idea? I don't want to cause any problems." "It's fine. Don't worry."

Luke and Logan finished unloading the car and went inside to unpack Logan's things and make dinner.

The two of them ran every morning together; Logan was quick and kept Luke at pace. One morning, they were running and Logan suddenly stopped. "Did you see that?" "What?" "I thought I saw someone running through the woods." "Probably another runner." "No, he was wearing a dark hoodie. In this heat? It's weird." Luke shrugged it off and kept running. They ran for an hour and when they returned, Logan's car windows had been smashed out. All of them. "Oh my god! Look at this! My windows! All of my windows!" "Probably some crack-heads." I'll take care of it. Don't worry." "Yeah, but why all the windows? Don't they usually just break one?" "Guess they were hitting it extra hard last night." They called the police and made the report so Luke's insurance would cover it. "See? All taken care of." "Seems weird though." "Stop worrying. These things happen here sometimes."

It was the third year since the death of Luke's parents. Luke always took this day to visit the family mausoleum. Luke walked to Logan's door, "I'll be home later tonight. Wanna grab dinner?" He didn't respond. Logan had missed their run that morning, so Luke figured he was just tired and wanted to sleep in, so Luke left a note on the counter and left. When Logan woke up he found the note on the counter next to the French-press. It was a beautiful day, the sun was shining and the sky was clear, enticing Logan to go outback and sunbathe. The sun on his naked flesh relaxed him as he fell asleep. He woke up to a car door slamming. It was coming from Walt's driveway. Logan looked over the fence, but couldn't see through the bushes that lined Walt's drive. Logan was afraid of Walt, but his curiosity got the best of him and he quickly dressed to go and investigate. As he walked down the back alley towards Walt's drive, he saw Walt carrying something heavy into the house. A shiver ran down Logan's spine. Whatever it was, Logan could only see that it was long and looked heavy, even for the massive man that was carrying it. What is that? He panicked. He wasn't sure why, but he felt something was not right.

He called Luke's phone, but it went straight to voicemail. Logan left several messages, but Luke never called back. Luke always answered his calls. Logan became increasingly worried and decided to call the police, but they wouldn't do anything for him. It had only been twelve hours and since he was an adult, they figured he had just decided to leave or was out somewhere. Besides, Logan wasn't family and had no connection to Luke other than friendship. Logan's imagination went wild as he thought the worst. Logan drove around Midtown all night looking for Luke. He drove past their local hangouts and walked through the park in hopes of finding Luke. Logan decided to come back to the house in hopes that Luke would have already returned, but the house was empty. Logan sat in the living room calling Luke's phone over and over again, hoping Luke would eventually pick up. Logan woke up late the next morning, expecting Luke to be sleeping in bed. He ran through the house, looking in every room, and found no Luke. He could only think of one place Luke could be, Walt's.

He gathered his courage and walked over to Walt's and knocked on the door. Nothing. He rang the doorbell three times. Finally, he saw a shadow come from the back of the house and walk towards the door. Walt opened the door in nothing but a black pair of leather shorts. "Yes. Can I help you?" "Uh- Is Luke here? I haven't heard from him all day. I thought he might be..." "Oh, you're Logan, right?" "I am. Have you seen Luke?" "Come in, come in. Don't want everyone to see me half-naked." Walt was filling out those leather shorts and Logan couldn't help but stare. "You like?" Walt rubbed himself and licked his lips. "Yes, but..." "Let's play." Logan found himself following Walt to the back of the house. The house was barely lit except the light coming from the basement. Walt had blackout curtain drawn on almost every window.

"I really wanted to know if you had seen Luke? He was supposed to be back..." "Don't you know that this is our anniversary?" "Don't you mean the anniversary of his parent's death?" "Yes, but also the same time we fell in love. We helped each other grow, he freed me. He usually disappears for a day or two around this time. You would understand that better if you were truly close to him, like I am. You may never know. Drink?" "I -uh...don't think..." "It's ok. I am sorry I came across so intense when you first moved in. I am just very protective of my boy." "It's ok. I can see why he loved you." Walt strutted towards the refrigerator, "Beer?" "Sure. Thank you." Walt walked the beer over to Logan, "Here ya go." Logan nervously took it from his hands; their fingers lingered.

Logan felt Walt's massive hands pressing against him. Logan reached out; his sweaty hands slid over the leather, feeling Walt's massive endowment grow under his touch. Walt's body felt strong and powerful, bringing Logan to his knees. Walt grabbed onto Logan and drew him in close. Walt had Logan in his grip as they kissed. He pinned Logan against the fridge and made quick work to strip him and bring Logan to his attention. They gripped one another in a fury of sexual power. Logan couldn't resist man that gripped him. Walt leaned in, reaching behind Logan, gripping his cheeks, lifting Logan onto his fingers. Logan moaned and felt the massive member slide under him. Walt carried Logan to the counter, setting him on his stomach. Walt took no time in putting himself inside Logan, ripping him. Logan cried out, but found himself pinned under Walt's force. He struggled to free himself. Walt groaned after several agonizing minutes. He reached around Logan's throat with his massive biceps, squeezing harder and harder as he licked the back of Logan's neck, whispering, "now you're mine too." Logan fought with all his remaining strength but hadn't enough left. Walt's grip tightened and all went dark.

Logan woke up to discover that he was handcuffed to the chains on the wall, wearing nothing but a leather jock-strap and a ball-gag in his mouth. His body ached. The room was dark except the light hanging over the steel table. Luke was on it. Logan tried to scream and break free, but it was no use. Walt came in, "Ah. You're awake. Just in time." Logan leaned away from the wall, struggling to stand up. He couldn't believe his eyes. Walt had a steel cart with medical instruments on it next to where Luke was tied down with leather straps, spread-eagle over the steel table. "You boys are all the same. You see a man and think we are just something to play with, something you can use to fulfill you. What about our needs? What about how you fulfill us? You can't just take it away once you give a little." Luke had begun to wake up. Tears fell from his eyes as he looked to Logan, trying to talk through his ball-gag. "You are so sweet my boy. So delicious." Walt ran his hands over Luke's body, stopping at his thighs. "Yes. This is it."

Walt grabbed the scalpel from the tray. The young men stared at each other, shaking violently. "Hold still. You don't want me to hit an artery." Walt sat on a steel stool, still in his leather shorts. He put on black leather gloves and made his first incision. Luke's eyes bulged as he screamed through the gag and then passed out. Walt sliced Luke's thigh open pulling the tissue back, exposing the layers of muscles. Walt sat there and explained his procedure to Logan like he was giving a lecture in a hospital theatre. "The first incision is always the most important. Notice how the layers of flesh separate as you pull away from the sub-dermis? Tonight we are going to try the Rectus femoris. This muscle is easily recognizable. See the outline? Now it is important not to cut the Femoral or the Deep femoral arteries. He'll bleed out if we do." Logan vomited and puke spewed around the gag and through his nose. Walt carefully sliced the muscle from Luke's thigh, exposing the femur and laid it out on a clean steel cart. "Looks like a pork tenderloin. Doesn't it?" Walt rolled the cart toward Logan. "I want you to try this. I will let you go if you do." Logan was sobbing, but shook his head in agreement. He tried to muffle the anguish, but vomited again. "Stop that! You're making a mess of things." Walt cut a piece of the muscle and picked it up with his fingers. He lifted it into his mouth, blood dripping off of his lips. "Delicious. Now you." Walt removed Logan's ball gag, relieving the pressure that squeezed his face. Logan looked at Luke who wasn't moving and stared Walt in the face, spitting on him. "You're a monster!" Walt chuckled and cut a big piece for Logan. He caressed Logan's torso with it, drawing a blood line straight up to his mouth. "Take it!" Logan shook and slowly opened his mouth. He sobbed and chewed. "Well?" "Tastes like pennies." Walt laughed violently as he walked away, leaving the young men alone with their fears. Luke woke up screaming through his ball-gag and Walt returned to sew and bandage Luke's thigh up. "Good boy. You did so well. The pain will subside soon. By the way, Logan thinks you are delicious!" Walt swung the light to strobe over Logan as he stood chained to the wall, revealing the trail of blood that led to his mouth. Vomit spewed from Luke's nose and around the gag. Walt attended to the mess, never allowing the smell of death to enter their nightmares.

He left them alone in the dark for what seemed like days before he returned. They could only hear each other's muffled speech through the dark basement and the clanking of the chains as Logan tried to free himself. Walt came and went for weeks, exchanging the boys' positions from the wall to the table, feeding them from one another, giving them water, bathing them to keep their wounds clean. Walt made use of the boys' position and took great pleasure in using their bodies for his sexual hunger. He raped them over and over, taking a piece of their sanity with every thrust.

Luke filled with rage with each piece of meat he was forced to eat. Walt assumed them to be too weak to try anything and let his guard down, allowing Luke to grab a scalpel from the cart as he was being lifted up from the steel table. Luke was leaning against Walt's massive body as he was being placed into his chains and a power surged within him, a powerful force like that of the Seti Gandaki River. He lifted his arms behind Walt and stabbed with all his might. The scalpel sliced into Walt's bulging deltoid, causing Walt to drop him and retract from the wall. Luke fell to the ground, his weak body struggling to lift itself up. Walt was stunned by the sudden act of resistance. Luke sat on his knees and stabbed into Walt's lower abdomen. Walt collapsed. Luke drew on the remaining strength left within his body and cut the harness that Walt had laid Logan in while he transferred Luke to the wall. Logan fell to the ground, but gathered his strength and the two slowly climbed the staircase towards the blinding light of day, leaving Walt to bleed out on the cold basement floor.

The men yelled with ferocity and blood-curdling screams that drew out the neighbors to investigate. One man puked when he saw the state of the two young men as they dragged their naked bodies down the drive. Stitches lay over concave portions of their bodies where muscle had once been. They clawed their way towards freedom from that dungeon, down the drive towards the street, collapsing when someone put a blanket around them. Sirens blared in the distance. The police arrived and quickly went to the basement, guns drawn. They rushed down the stairs to discover nothing but a puddle of blood.

The A.P.D. canvassed the area and led a manhunt that turned up nothing, no traces of Walt. The police report recounted the horrific tortures of their account. The police chief recognized this as the most gory and extensive case he had ever encountered. The neighborhood quietly acknowledged the events that took place, closing one another off. Everyone remained in a state of limbo, wondering where Walt had escaped to and if he would return. Their lives, however distant from this event, were changed forever. Neighbors who had known each other for years, stopped saying hello to one another, only exchanging nervous glances from their driveways.

Luke and Logan were rushed to Crawford Long Hospital and sedated while the doctors looked over the wounds of the young men. Walt's precision methods had left the wounds in healthy shape with the exception of their loss of body mass. Luke regained his strength after days in the I.C.U, but Logan was not so lucky. The shock of the events had drained him beyond recovery and he passed away on the third day in recovery. Luke came to and discovered a delivery of red roses had shown up in his room. He took the out the card and read the single word written in red ink, "Delicious!"

Justin Fredericksen is a Seattle native, calling Atlanta home. This 37 year old writer is currently working towards his MFA at SCAD. Justin's work breaks heteronormative expectations in Fiction by including the LGBT community in the horrors Fiction has to offer.

THE BONY LEGGED
MARIA WOLFE

Catherine's mother heard from her Realtor friend that an old lady was moving to Liberty Court. Everyone was gossiping about it, but no one knew anything. All the kids on the cul-de-sac were mad—the woman bought the empty lot between the Wilsons' and the Rothmans' where they played baseball and kickball and tag. But Catherine didn't care. At age twelve, she was much too mature to take part in such silly games.

Early one Saturday morning, a fiercely-barking dog woke Catherine from a sound sleep. Dogs never barked that loudly on Liberty Court; the Home Owners' Association expressly forbade it. Catherine grumbled over to her bedroom window to investigate. When she raised the blinds, her mouth gaped at the sight: in the space across the street that, the night before, had been a mess of uncut green grass and cast-off toys, a two-storied house with a two-car garage had appeared.

Catherine screwed her eyes shut before looking again. No, she was not dreaming. The new house stood on two large chicken legs, towering over its neighbors. The muscular, white-feathered thighs ended in yellow-scaled feet with large, nasty-sharp claws. A bleached-white picket fence penned in the now-dead-brown yard. Parked on the dirt driveway was a metal mortar, much too big for grinding spices but just right for carrying an adult; a pestle leaned against its side. Thick, black smoke spewed from the red-brick chimney, clouding the neighborhood sky.

Last night, the new house must have strolled over to Liberty Court on those chicken legs. But houses, Catherine knew for a fact, didn't travel around on chicken legs. This was the suburbs, not some make-believe fairy tale with heroes and monsters. And picket fences certainly didn't show up out of nowhere, not without prior authorization from the Home Owners' Association.

The house scratched at the ground with one of its clawed chicken feet.

With a gasp, Catherine jumped back from the window. The lift cord slipped out of her hand, and the blinds fell with a shuffle and a bang. She spun around and sprinted downstairs to check on her little brother.

Catherine smelled the burnt pancake before she reached the kitchen. Her mother was mumbling over a sputtering skillet, a spatula in her hand. A smoky haze hung over the room. At the kitchen table, Ivan readied his plastic toy soldiers for deployment. Her little brother disliked pancakes and ignored the blackened one on his plate.

"Mom?" Catherine glared at her mother's latest boyfriend as he forced chunks of produce into the feed tube of his masticating juicer. The pancakes were special for him. "Mom," she yelled over the groaning machine. Rick wouldn't be around for long, she bet.

"What? What is it, Catherine?" Her mother slid the spatula beneath a cooking pancake. When she withdrew the utensil, batter covered it. "Dammit. Look what you made me do."

"The old lady moved in. Come see." She dragged her mother into the living room. Ivan trailed behind Catherine, a toy soldier grasped in each hand.

With the green curtains drawn, the picture window perfectly framed the new house, now dancing on its chicken legs, across the street.

"Goddammit." Her mother threw the spatula onto the carpet, just as the smoke alarm went off. "That's really gonna fuck up our property values."

***

At noon, the adults convened an emergency barbecue in the Martins' backyard to discuss their new neighbor. Even Catherine's mother was invited, despite her ugly feud with the Home Owners' Association over her minimalist lawn care and lackadaisical home maintenance. Rick came, too; he had been spending a lot of time at Catherine's house. In front of everyone, he draped his arm around her mother's shoulders until Catherine towed her away for her own good.

A slab of ribs sizzled on the grill in Mr. Martin's newly installed outdoor kitchen. On a nearby granite countertop, Mrs. Martin arranged colorful plastic bowls of side dishes that the neighborhood wives had made. Catherine's mother contributed a lemon pasta salad, still in its grocery-store container, but, this time, Mrs. Martin didn't mutter any nasty comments about her poor homemaking skills.

All the kids from the cul-de-sac were at the barbecue, but none of them felt like playing. Though it was late August, they shivered in their hoodies and jeans. The smoke-laden air was thick with misery.

Even at age twelve, Catherine was turned away from the table with the adults. Her mother pointed her to a distant spot on the well-manicured lawn. Alone, Catherine sat cross-legged on a large beach towel unfurled on the ground, picking at a cheeseburger that bled ketchup and mustard. Her paper plate was soggy with potato salad. She had no appetite for lunch.

Torches lit the murky backyard, the flames casting shifting patterns of darkness and light. The grown-ups batted around low, urgent words like a tetherball. Catherine strained to listen over the confusion of children's voices from the picnic blankets around her.

But then Estelle, Mr. Martin's mother-in-law, leaped up from her lawn chair to speak. She lived with the Martins in their basement bedroom and taught the kids of Liberty Court Spanish curse words. Mrs. Martin urged her mother back into her seat—no one knew what would pop out of Estelle's mouth—but Estelle swatted her away with a wrinkled hand.

"That fence," Estelle said in her booming voice, ignoring the shushing from her daughter, "I saw it up close during my power walk this morning. Made my best time cause I was scared shitless." She wagged her finger. "It's made of bones. Human bones, I tell you. Femurs and tibias, I'd wager. Maybe some fibulas but coulda been a bunch of humeri instead."

The adults hopped up from their seats and shook their fists in the direction of the new house. From her beach towel, Catherine overheard their angry whisper-shouts: human sacrifice, witchcraft, non-HOA compliant fencing. Mr. Martin climbed onto a bench and conducted everyone in the familiar chant: "HOA, HOA, HOA." Even Catherine's mother joined in. Rick, too.

"H-O-A." Catherine fake-formed the letters to placate Mr. Martin and the neighbors. She couldn't say it aloud, not when her family was also a frequent HOA target. The group grew louder, more furious. "HOA, HOA, HOA," they roared. Still, she could make out the raspy yips of the Martins' dog as he crouched behind the screen of their patio door; since the house appeared that morning, the dog hadn't stopped barking.

Catherine trembled but not from the cold: the chimney smoke had thickened, coloring the sky above them a charcoal black. But, when she looked toward Pine Street, it was a cloudless blue. The sun had only deserted Liberty Court.

***

The Welcoming Committee dropped in on the new neighbor that afternoon. An unauthorized fence made of human bones could not be tolerated, the Home Owners' Association had decided; their objections must be aired with the old lady. Mr. Wilson brought a copy of the thick HOA Guidelines along with his famous oatmeal raisin cookies; Mrs. Rothman carried a plastic container of her leftover, equally famous potato salad. Catherine peered from her living room window as Mr. Martin, the HOA president, led them along the sidewalk. The front gate screamed open, and the house squatted down on its chicken legs to meet the group.

Mr. Martin didn't have to ring the doorbell: the front door was ajar. Catherine couldn't see her, but the old woman was waiting.

First Mr. Martin disappeared into the house. Then Mr. Wilson. Before she entered, Mrs. Rothman paused to glance behind her at the crowd of neighbors gathered on Catherine's front lawn. From his beach chair, Mr. Rothman waved at his wife. "Go get 'er, honey," he bellowed before sipping from his third bottle of beer.

Though the lawn chairs and coolers cleared out after an hour, the Welcoming Committee only emerged later that evening. Catherine had already changed into her superhero pajamas but insisted on attending the HOA meeting at the Wilsons' house. The neighbors were shocked: Mr. Martin's thick, wavy hair had fallen out; Mr. Wilson was stuttering; and Mrs. Rothman had not only forgotten her award-winning potato salad recipe but also left her plastic container behind. The Committee members refused to speak of the visit except to say, "She calls herself Baba Yaga. The Bony Legged."

**

Danny Wilson wasn't in his bedroom when his parents woke up early on Sunday morning. He was neither inside the house nor outside in the shed. Since Mr. Wilson was still stuttering, Mrs. Wilson phoned the police and alerted the neighbors.

While Catherine peeked through the slats of the blinds in her bedroom, her mother and Rick rushed outside to console the Wilsons. The sun was rising over Pine Street but, under its cover of chimney smoke, the cul-de-sac was dark. On Liberty Court, the dusk-to-dawn outdoor floodlights were still shining brightly.

Police vans sped onto Liberty Court, sirens wailing, lights flashing. SWAT officers in helmets and body armor, their assault rifles at the ready, scrambled out. A group of neighbors, still in their pajamas and bathrobes, met them at the Wilsons' front curb. Mrs. Wilson spoke to the lead officer, all the while jabbing her finger toward Baba Yaga's house.

The SWAT team vaulted over the picket fence. The men surrounded the chicken-legged house, their rifles aimed and prepared to fire. The house backed away but stopped when a police officer with a megaphone instructed Baba Yaga to surrender.

The house sank to the ground, and the officers lowered their weapons. The old woman opened the front door and welcomed the team inside.

Several hours later, the SWAT officers rappelled from the front porch of the house as it paced around the fenced-in yard on its chicken legs. Catherine counted: of the team of ten, only nine departed. The surviving men rushed to their vehicles. The vans sped away from Liberty Court, sirens wailing, lights flashing.

The old woman wasn't with them. Nor was Danny Wilson.

The gathering of neighbors slipped away from the Wilsons and their grief. Alone in their driveway, Mrs. Wilson sobbed while Mr. Wilson, his face expressionless, held her.

Baba Yaga added more pickets to her fence that afternoon. A couple of femurs, Estelle later reported at the HOA meeting. Adult femurs picked clean of flesh.

The police were called but declined to come back to Liberty Court. "It's against department regulations after an officer has been eaten," the chief said. "Not without an internal review first."

The Wilsons put a "For Sale" sign on their now-lifeless front lawn. Danny still had a little brother for them to keep safe. The Wilsons moved out that day.

***

That week, the sky over Liberty Court remained a midnight black. The grass withered, the trees became naked husks. Only "For Sale" signs blossomed. The neighbors fled to friends and family. Once children had played outdoors; now the sidewalks and backyards were empty.

Catherine's family couldn't afford to leave. The kitchen had just been remodeled, and her mother had a mortgage with a high interest rate and student loans from her Masters' degree in Russian Literature. Instead, Catherine secured the house against Baba Yaga. An extra deadbolt appeared on the front door, then another on the back door. She posted stickers advertising their brand-new alarm system on the windows and doors.

Ivan resumed sleeping in Catherine's room, just like after their parents' divorce. Her brother had been a baby, too young to remember their father, but Catherine did. The drinking, the screaming, the slammed doors—the man had abandoned them even before he left. While her mother had fallen apart, Catherine took care of everything.

Rick stopped coming around. After she read his breakup text, Catherine's mother began to cry. "I thought he was different," she said to Catherine. "But he's just like your father. A huge disappointment."

Catherine shrugged. That was exactly what she had expected.

***

On Friday morning, Catherine's mother dressed in her power suit and high heels. She had an important meeting with her boss at the bank and couldn't drive Catherine and her brother to school.

"Go straight to the bus stop," her mother said to Catherine. The babysitter had just called to cancel—no one dared venture onto Liberty Court. Even Rick was too scared of Baba Yaga to retrieve his fancy juicer. "Don't stop. Don't look back."

Catherine sat at the kitchen table, eating a bowl of oatmeal and sipping a glass of fresh beet-kale juice. She wasn't worried: the mortar hadn't been parked across the street that morning.

Next to her, Ivan and his toy soldiers were attacking a building-block house standing on building-block chicken legs. He paused to gobble down the sugary loops in his cereal bowl. With a whack from his hand, the blocks clattered down. Ivan clapped: "Baba Yaga is dead!"

Her mother leaned down to kiss Catherine's forehead. "Take care of your little brother."

"Sure." She brushed off the imprint of her mother's lips. Catherine always took care of Ivan. "Okay, Mom."

"And Ivan, you be sure to mind your sister." Her mother hugged him to her belly. "Be a good boy." She smoothed down his blond hair where she had mussed it up.

As she turned away, Ivan seized her leg. "No, no, no. Don't leave me, Mommy," he bawled. His little fingers wouldn't let go. "Baba Yaga will steal me away just like Danny." With each of her steps toward the door to the garage, her mother dragged Ivan along the tile floor.

Catherine wrenched Ivan away. "We'll be fine," she said to her mother. "I'll protect Ivan. You go."

Her mother's red car backed out of the driveway as Catherine stared, her nose scrunched against the living room window. Her mother was wiping away her makeup along with her tears, but Catherine was dry-eyed.

As the red car approached the corner, the mortar flew onto Liberty Court. Catherine's mother honked and swerved to avoid it. Her car disappeared into the traffic of Pine Street while the mortar continued along the road toward the chicken-legged house.

Baba Yaga sat in the bowl of the mortar, steering with her rudder-like pestle. The noise of the pestle against the asphalt was a horror of a hundred dry-erase markers against a whiteboard. The old woman landed the vehicle in her driveway. Stuck to the side of the mortar was a bumper sticker: "I Brake for Animals."

A black caftan whirled around Baba Yaga's bony legs. Her smile had a metallic glint. The old woman waved before Catherine could duck behind the curtain.

Mierda, Catherine thought. Baba Yaga's back.

***

Catherine rushed along the sidewalk, eager to reach the safety of the bus stop on Pine Street. Her book-filled rucksack thumped against her back. She heard her brother's short breaths as he fought to keep up with her longer legs. He was only five years old, but he knew the danger; Danny Wilson had been his best friend.

Then Ivan was no longer beside her. "Don't look back," her mother had said, but Catherine spun around. Her brother was kneeling on the cracked sidewalk with his shoelaces undone. His fingers fumbled at making bunny-ears like Catherine had taught him. Tears streamed down his chubby face.

Catherine lifted her brother into her arms and hurried to the main road, just six driveways away. He was small, but she struggled with his weight. His tiny arms clutched at her heaving shoulders, his little legs at her waist.

The yellow school bus rumbled along Pine Street, toward its stop on the corner. She quickened her steps. Four driveways to go... They were so close.

She heard a howl coming from behind, like a knife being sharpened by the bearded old man at the grocery store. Catherine kept running, her straight brown hair streaming in the wind. Ivan hid his face against her neck and whimpered. Two driveways... The dreadful noise grew louder.

Darkness dropped over them. Catherine punched and kicked at the rough cloth sack that had swallowed her and Ivan. The stench of onions was overpowering. The bag was hoisted up. Together, Catherine and Ivan tumbled to its bottom. Her brother wailed her name and squeezed her tighter.

Inside the bag, they bounced again and again against a hard surface. Footsteps padded. Hinges creaked open, then closed. When the bag fell to the ground, Catherine was knocked apart from Ivan. He let out a strangled cry. She slapped away the lax cloth to find him. Her hand touched his arm.

"Little ones," an ancient voice said, "come out of the sack."

Catherine whispered to Ivan, "It's going to be okay," but she was lying; it hadn't been okay for Danny Wilson. She crawled out of the bag into a dim room. Ivan followed Catherine through the mouth of the sack, the burlap sliding to the ground behind him like a snake regurgitating its prey. She pushed her brother behind her. He grabbed her hand.

Baba Yaga filled the open-concept kitchen. Her terrible head with its iron teeth bumped against the pendant light fixture. Each bony leg with its orthopedic shoe-clad foot occupied a different corner of the room. She reeked of mothballs and mold.

"Little ones," Baba Yaga said, "I must leave you to gather more wood for my stove." Her gray teeth flashed as she smiled. "Then I will eat you both and suck the marrow from your bones."

The massive door shut behind Baba Yaga. Catherine and her brother were trapped.

Catherine searched the entire house. The doors were bolted. She couldn't force them open. Bars blocked the blacked-out windows. She couldn't bend them apart. The cabinets and drawers were padlocked. She couldn't break the locks.

She slumped onto a chair in the formal dining room. Her chin quivered as she fought her despair. "If only I could save Ivan..." Catherine had always protected her little brother from bad dreams and bullies. Impossible this time—she'd found no weapon to defeat the witch, no route to break out. "I'd do anything."

When she shuffled back to the kitchen, Ivan was huddled on the bamboo floor, his face hidden against his bent legs. Catherine stooped to stroke his shaking back. At least he couldn't see the broken bones scattered on the poured-concrete countertop. Or the large, black cast-iron stove, opposite the farmhouse-style kitchen sink.

Over Ivan's sobs, Catherine heard a squeak. Then another.

A white lab rat scurried across the room and onto Ivan's foot. "Wipe away your tears, child," the rat said in a formal tone. "All is not lost. The house heard your sister's plea and sent me."

Stopping mid-sob, Ivan raised his head to stare at the rodent perched on his shoe. "Catherine, that rat is talking." He wiped his runny nose on his sleeve and grinned, his fears forgotten. "Can I keep him?"

Catherine shook her head. A talking rat was just as nonsensical as a cannibalistic old woman and a large, flying mortar. "No, Ivan. Not without his permission."

"Thank you, child. That is more autonomy than Baba Yaga has ever accorded me." The rat ground his front teeth. His red eyes bulged. "She gave me the ability to speak but threatens me if I use it. Like the house, I am merely her unwilling servant."

With a giggle of delight, Ivan scooped up the rodent and clasped him against his chest. The rat hissed.

"Let him go, Ivan," Catherine said. Her brother frowned but loosened his hold. The rat wiggled free.

The rat's long tail swished over the floor. "Children, if you give me food, I will assist you." He drew back his small pink ears. "After I denounced her murderous conduct, that witch Baba Yaga ceased to feed me. She would not even share Mrs. Rothman's famous potato salad."

Catherine rummaged through her backpack and handed the rat her pita with hummus and her carrot sticks. She would be dead by lunchtime, she figured, and wouldn't need the food. The rat refused the bag of artisanal cookies—since Baba Yaga had rescued him from the Obesity Research Lab at the University, he couldn't tolerate sweets.

In exchange, the rat brought her a stained, white hand towel; a brush matted with wiry, gray hair; and a comb missing several teeth. "These are magical objects that will aid in your escape." He nibbled at a carrot stick dipped in hummus. "Baba Yaga enchanted them, to support the fight for animal rights."

For Ivan's sake, Catherine hoped that the rat was right. But she didn't believe in magic, just like she didn't believe in happy endings.

***

Hours passed before Baba Yaga returned. The burlap sack over her shoulder was heavy with firewood. The old woman ignored Catherine and her brother as she loaded the wood into the vintage stove. The flames became hotter and brighter.

A muttered spell unlocked the kitchen cabinetry. Baba Yaga removed a large roasting pan from a base cabinet. She added large-diced potatoes and carrots and onions to the pan.

The old woman placed the pan on the ledge in front of the open stove door. Pointing at Ivan, she said, "Get in."

Catherine stepped in front of her brother. "No." That was not what she had planned. "I'll go first."

"Yes, yes, yes. You will taste much better than your brother, little one." Baba Yaga pinched Catherine's arm. "There's more meat to chomp from your bones." She cackled. "And perhaps you are tall enough to provide two more pickets for my lovely fence."

Catherine settled into the pan. "Oh, no," she said. "I'm not such a little one, it seems." Her legs didn't fit inside the roaster: one pointed straight up, the other straight down.

The old woman gnashed her metal teeth. "No," she shouted. "You will not go into the stove that way. Do it again."

Catherine switched her legs. "Oh, no," she said. "This isn't any better." Now one pointed straight down, the other straight up.

"No," Baba Yaga yelled. Her gray hair crackled with electricity. "Not like that. Do it again."

Again, Catherine adjusted her legs. "Oh, no," she said. "I just can't get it right." Both pointed straight out of the pan.

Baba Yaga tossed Catherine from the roaster. The potatoes and carrots and onions fell with her onto the floor. "No!" The witch arranged herself in the pan, her spindly arms and bony legs tucked inside. "This is how you do it."

Catherine shot up from the floor and shoved the roasting pan into the hot stove. Ivan slammed the stove door shut.

Baba Yaga screeched and pounded against the cast iron.

Catherine grabbed her backpack and her brother's hand. The rat climbed from the backpack onto her shoulder, his claws digging into the fabric of her hoodie.

"Hurry, children. The flames in the stove will not kill Baba Yaga," the rat said. "She is a magical creature and must die by magic."

The front door opened for the children, and the house squatted down. "The house wants to help," the rat had told them, "despite the risk. It never wanted sentience or giant chicken legs. All it yearns for is to be a normal house once again."

The children raced from Baba Yaga as fast as they could.

Metal ground against the road. Catherine looked over her shoulder. Baba Yaga was behind them, flying in her mortar. The stove hadn't harmed her.

Catherine took the rat's dirty towel from her backpack and threw it to the ground. A wide river appeared, stretching beyond Liberty Court. Baba Yaga couldn't fly her mortar above its turbulent currents. She stopped to slurp the waters dry.

The children sprinted by the Wilsons' house, then the Martins' house. Ivan was panting, but he didn't fall behind.

Metal scraped against the pavement. Catherine looked over her shoulder. Baba Yaga was again behind them, flying in her mortar. The river hadn't slowed her.

Catherine took the rat's hairbrush and flung it at the ground. The sidewalks crumbled, the road cracked, and a thick forest sprang up. Baba Yaga couldn't pass her mortar between the trees. She stopped to gnaw the wood to splinters with her sharp, iron teeth.

Pine Street was busy with cars. Catherine stood at the corner of Liberty and Pine with her arm across Ivan's chest. When the pedestrian signal displayed the walking man, she pulled her brother across the road.

Baba Yaga was coming, and Catherine let her approach. Closer. The old woman was bent forward in her seat. Closer. Her head was thrown back as she cackled. Closer. The mortar accelerated. Closer. The shrill scream of the pestle grating against the road was deafening. Ivan clamped his hands over his ears.

Almost...

Catherine took the rat's comb and hurled it to the ground. It landed in the middle of the street, right in front of Baba Yaga and her mortar. A wall of fire exploded up toward the sky.

Even from the sidewalk, Catherine shied away from the intense heat. Cars entering the intersection honked and skidded away.

Baba Yaga couldn't fly over the fiery barrier. She couldn't fly around it. Her pestle-brake squealed, but it was too late. Shrieking, the old woman and her mortar barreled into the enchanted flames.

Caught in the blaze, the witch, Baba Yaga, burned.

***

With Baba Yaga's death, the night-cloud over Liberty Court vanished. Grass grew, trees sprouted. Catherine's mother sent a group text, and the neighbors returned. The "For Sale" signs were discarded. Children swarmed the broken sidewalks and waterlogged backyards. Splinters of wood carpeted the road, and all the kids on the cul-de-sac were mad—it was barefoot weather, yet they had to wear shoes.

Mr. Martin, as the president of the Home Owners' Association, organized an emergency barbecue to celebrate. He and Mr. Wilson spent the morning of the party at Baba Yaga's house, wielding a chainsaw. Their eyes were wide and wild. Snarls deformed their faces, making them grotesque.

"Please, please don't kill the house," Catherine begged. She stood between it and the two men, her arms spread wide. "The house helped save me and Ivan." Now she had to defend it. "It didn't hurt anyone. It had been a normal house until Baba Yaga enslaved it, and it hated her for that."

But the two men didn't care. "Baba Yaga murdered my son," Mr. Wilson yelled. Behind him, Mr. Martin began yanking on the starter rope to get the chainsaw running. "Because of your meddling, I can't kill that goddamned witch. But someone must pay."

"Don't punish the house because I killed Baba Yaga." Catherine pulled on Mr. Wilson's arm. "I didn't want to do it. But I had to. For Ivan."

Mr. Wilson shoved Catherine aside, and she stumbled to the ground. "I will have vengeance, little girl."

Catherine clambered to her feet. "This is wrong," she said to the rodent sitting on her shoulder. "I have to stop them."

"No, child," the rat said, his voice low so no one would suspect his magical gift of speech. His long whiskers twitched. "Look at them. These men are beyond reason. They will dispatch us both if you again intervene."

The house tried to flee on its chicken legs but, the rat whispered to Catherine, it couldn't escape the enchantments that imprisoned it within the fenced-in yard. The two men cornered the house. Terror radiated from its two stories. Its windows banged open and closed.

The chainsaw sputter-buzzed through the chicken feathers and flesh. When the chainsaw failed, the two men hacked at the legs with axes. Blood saturated their clothes and dripped from their hands.

For hours, Catherine witnessed the dismemberment though she wanted to scurry to her bedroom and hide with Ivan under the covers. She had to look; otherwise, no one would remember the bravery of the poor house. The rat buried his head in her long hair, letting only one red eye peek out: the house had been his only friend.

Finally, Baba Yaga's house, separated from its chicken legs, crashed onto the ground. Its mouthless screams faded, replaced by the wild cheers of the frenzied neighbors crowded onto the street. The loudest shouts came from Catherine's mother despite her knowing the true story of the house. Catherine heard it all, even with her palms pressed against her ears.

Mrs. Rothman washed the blood away with her garden hose while Danny Wilson's mother gathered the red-stained white feathers in large yard waste bags. Mrs. Martin butchered the meat, slicing it from the bones. Estelle carted the chicken feet away in a wheelbarrow; "the yellow," she said, "matches the decor in my basement bedroom." The kids knocked down the picket fence and threw the bones into a truck sent by the University.

That night, the neighbors feasted on chicken. The stench of grilling meat clouded the air. Dark red barbecue sauce smeared their voracious mouths and savage fingers. The neighbors broke the chicken bones and sucked out the marrow. They circled and jeered the burning carcass of the once magic house. Catherine's mother joined them. Rick, too—he had slithered back to their house on Liberty Court, and her mother allowed it. That was exactly what Catherine had expected from her mother—a huge disappointment.

Catherine refused to take part in their cruel celebration. She, Ivan, and the talking rat sat alone on a beach towel and shared lemon pasta salad from the grocery store. Everyone glared and grumbled at her. "This is a happy ending," they all declared. But, as the hero who had slain the evil witch, Catherine knew better: this story had no "happily ever after."

Monsters still lived on Liberty Court, no matter what the neighbors said.

Maria Wolfe lives and writes in northeast Ohio, where she also practiced as a surgeon. Her fiction has appeared in The Examined Life Journal, Please See Me, and Coffin Bell. She is currently working on a novel.

A LOSS OF APPETITE
TRIPP DURDEN

The harsh blue lights of the police cruisers assault Brady's senses as he gets out of his car. Even when he turns away from them, towards his destination, he is plagued with phantom flashes that look like multicolored ghosts haunting his vision. He pauses for a moment allowing the visions to pass before taking it all in, attempting to establish a solid mental image for when he is describing it later. His breath makes clouds of vapor that float in front of him in the dark. The ghosts in another form, after him again. They hang lazily in the air until he walks through them, vanquishing them as he goes. Above him, the moon is almost non existent except for the tiniest pen knife sliver. The stars are bright in the winter sky above him. It is cold and only going to get colder.

Double checking that he has his pen and notebook, He makes his way forward through the cold and towards the crime scene. He flashes his media badge to the officers on the edge of the site letting them know without a word that he belongs here. Cops tended to be protective of crime scenes. It wouldn't do to be mistaken for an imposter. In his mind, he can see an officer pulling his gun. He fires once...twice...thrice. Now two dead bodies lie in the red colored mud. The officer to his left, a tall young cop with a pockmarked face, lifts the garish yellow crime scene tape to let him through. Brady reluctantly ducks beneath the would be dividing line and enters a world of nightmares.

Twenty feet in front of him lays the body of young woman, naked and exposed to the cold. She is lying face down in the muck at the bottom of a small embankment. The skin on her legs is a mottled purplish blue, almost the same color as the phantoms that were left

72

over from the cruiser lights. Whether this was from the temperature or from something more sinister, Brady is not sure. Her hair is matted with blood, bits of flesh, and what appear to be skull fragments. In his head, Brady attempts what his therapist calls "mental reframing". He tries to restructure the way in which he was interpreting the information that is flooding in through his eyes. Turning away from the body for a moment, he decides to pretend that they are snowflakes and nothing more. It is pretty cold out here. "It could have snowed a little." He thinks. Except, Brady knows that, even as cold as it is, it does not often snow in Georgia during November. With his stomach rolling and his gut threatening to stage a coup d'etat against the rest of his body, he turns his attention back to the dead girl.

Her back is covered in wounds that lay in a haphazard indistinguishable pattern. Combined with the almost black-not quite red-dried blood, it looks like a toddler had drawn on her with the world's sharpest ink pen. He tries to count the wounds and loses track. He notices an African-American woman standing near her, talking with a fellow officer. She seems at ease with the situation. Like she has done this, and seen this, one hundred times or more. "She probably has." Brady thinks before forcing himself to return his eyes to the horror show in front of him.

The woman's arms are bent and twisted at unnatural angles, the left one is mangled in such a way that even though her back faces Brady, it looks like she is waving hello to him. As if she might have been playing the part of gracious host at a house party.

"Hello, Brady! Welcome to the party! Thanks for coming on such short notice. Sorry that I didn't have more time to clean myself up for you! I have been absolutely killing myself in order to get this place ready in time!"

Brady shivers in a way that is distinctly different from how one shivers due to temperature. It's as if someone has stabbed him with an icicle directly in the gut. He can feel it all through his body. It crawls up his back to the base of his neck. It's as if one of the phantoms, the ones from the lights and the fog of his breath, has come to roost in his very soul. He is no longer in control. He wants to turn away but can't. He knows he should be taking notes but does not know where to begin. His eyes are trapped, as if locked there by some unseen magnetic force- as if the phantom possessing him is interested in this one thing- to the girl's left hand. Her ring finger has been torn completely off.

"You must be Brady!"

Brady jumps at the sound of the man's voice, cowering away from it like a child might cower away from the sound of thunder on a stormy night. The man chuckles as Brady composes himself enough to accept the extended hand the man has offered for a shake.

"The chief told me the paper would be sending you. My name is Officer Janikowski. I'll answer any questions you might have about our little lady over there." Janikowski says as he gestures towards the body. He is a large man but not exactly overweight. Hearty. Corn fed. Something along those lines. He wears his police hat slightly askew so that his receding hairline just barely peeks out from beneath it. His face is broad and bracketed with deep smile lines on each side. His face is covered in freckles. He shakes Brady's hand vigorously and then rests his hand on the butt of his gun in a lazy, force of habit way.

"Before we get started, you mind if I ask you a question?" Officer Janikowski asks while Brady readies his notebook.

"Sure thing." Brady replies declining to mention that he had indeed already asked him a question. He expects the heavy set man to have a question regarding something to do with a past story in the paper or maybe an inquiry as to what Brady is looking to get from his visit to tonight's crime scene.

"What do you call a reporter that doesn't know when to take a hike?"

"Huh?" Brady responds, a confused look appearing on his face.

"I said, what do you call a reporter that doesn't know when to take a hike?"

"Is he fucking with me? A shitty joke... now?" Brady thinks to himself. He glances back at the dead body in an attempt to remind the officer of their current situation before motioning to Janikowski that he doesn't know the answer with a shrug of his shoulders.

"A News-ance!" Janikowski exclaims as his face lights up with a clever smile. The man begins laughing, his face becomes a tomato, and he throws his head back as if howling at the moon.

Brady stands there. A little shocked. Confused.

"C'mon man. A NEWS-ance? A Nuisance?" The officer says looking at Brady expectantly. Waiting for him to start laughing hysterically.

"Oh. A nuisance. Yeah, that's pretty good." Brady says, mentally reminding himself how important it is to be on the good side of cops when you are a member of the media. "It took me a second, sorry!"

Janikowski scratches his head, clearly put off and wondering why someone might not laugh at a horrid pun joke while standing just feet away from a murder victim. Brady forges forward.

"So... is it her?" He asks, nodding his head back towards the dead girl.

"Yep. It is. We found her just a few hours ago." Janikowski says. He picks a piece of fuzz from the front of his uniform and flicks it into the wind. "Her parents have been notified and will be here to identify the body soon but all of that is just a formality, if you ask me."

"Heather Harris. Found close to 7 pm, just outside of Atlanta city limits. Parents will confirm identity." Brady scribbles quickly across the white surface of his notebook, marking the pristine surface with his ball point pen in a dark scratchy slashes that remind him of the girls wounds.

"What other details can you give me?" Brady asks without looking up from the paper.

Janikowski sniffs and rubs his hand in an upward motion from the bottom of his nose and over the tip. His hand leaves his face with a small wet spot on it. Brady's nose has began to leak as well.

"She was tortured, for sure. Her body has over one hundred lacerations to the torso alone. Her head was crushed on one side by a blunt object. We assume this was the injury that caused her death. It could have been a baseball bat but was probably something metal like a hammer." Janikowski says while Brady takes his notes. "In any case, the motherfucker using the hammer must have been swinging for the fences. Mark McGuire on the 'roids shit, ya know what I mean?" Janikowski mimes swinging a baseball bat as he says this. Brady stands dumbfounded.

"Anything else?"

"We were actually still doing some field work when you showed up, Brady boy. Let's go a little closer and I'll see what else we've learned."

Brady follows the detective towards the edge of the embankment. There are cops everywhere. They mill around like ants. Some are obviously busy with forensic work while others seem lost and looking for a task to complete. A man carrying a brown paper sack calls out to Janikowski.

"Ay, Steve! I gotchu a Hoagie from Brennan's. Hot peppers and all that!"

The man tosses the hoagie through the air like a football. Janikowski catches it, tucks it under his arm and pretends to stiff arm a would be tackler. The man is clearly fond of pretending to be a sports star.

"Thanks, Reynolds. I owe ya one. I'm friggin' starving." Janikowski says as he unwraps the foil from the sandwich and immediately dives in.

Down the embankment, next to the body, a forensic agent with an afro puff squats in the mud. Her black field shoes are sunk two inches deep. Brady notices her pants leg is barely touching the leg of the woman. She is wearing gloves and is inspecting the space between the girls thighs, directly beneath her anus. This is the closest Brady has been to a dead body in his entire life outside of a funeral. He can smell something horrid but refuses to allow himself to acknowledge what the source is. Instead, he busies himself with scribbling a description of his surroundings in his note for later.

Janikowski seems to take no notice of the smell and continues eating.

"What ya got for me, Emeonye?" He asks through a mouthful of Italian bread, hot peppers, and assorted meats.

"She was definitely sexually molested. Whether it was rape or not? I don't know. So far, we have found no seminal fluid but, you never know. Here's to hoping." She says as she runs her hands down the inside of Heather Harris' leg.

"Any clue as to how long she has been dead?" Brady asks her, half expecting her to ignore him. Instead, she snaps an answer off immediately.

"She died from blunt force trauma somewhere close to four days ago based on the rate of decay we see. It seems all of her other injuries were sustained before then, including the broken arms, except for one."

"And which injury, pray tell, is that?" Detective Janikowski asks her looking over at Brady and spinning his finger in a circle next to his temple in the international sign for insane. He is still munching his hoagie.

"The missing ring finger. It is by far the freshest injury. It seems to have been removed post mortem. I believe whoever her killer was had a personal, specific reason for doing so. Perhaps it was to get the engagement ring? Speaking of rings on fingers, Have they located the fiancee?" she asks, placing her hand in a particularly private spot on the body in front of her.

Janikowski lets out a small burp before answering her question. Brady rolls his eyes. "This guy is unbelievable."

"Oh, yeah. Chief Riggins has him at the station now. He has been suspect number one you know. He ain't going nowhere no time soon. Say, Brady, What exactly is-"

Janikowski is interrupted by a triumphant shout from Detective Emeonye as she removes her hand from Heather's private areas and holds something aloft.

"Welp. I guess whoever cut her finger off didn't want the ring." she says holding out her hand.

In her outstretched palm lies the severed ring finger of Heather Harris. The diamond ring bloodied and smudged with grime still wrapped tightly around the small digit.

"Was that.. inside her?" Brady asks with a gag tagged on the end like an exclamation point.

"It was indeed." Replies the stoic Black woman. Holding the finger out for everyone to see, she resembles an angel of death, proudly displaying a souvenir in the middle of a muddy battlefield, instead of a cop working a case just outside of Atlanta.

"Jesus Christ." Says Janikowski with a tremble to his voice. "I think I'm gonna puke."

Brady chuckles grimly and turns to the middle aged police officer.

"I guess even you have your limits, eh Janikowski? A finger up the ass is all it takes, huh?" He asks finding a weird sense of pleasure knowing the blowhard officer is finally as bothered by the scene as he is.

Janikowski is bent over heaving, his sandwich dropped and forgotten on the ground beside him. After he has expunged the recently devoured hoagie, he recovers and turns on Brady.

"Easy kid. I ain't no spring chicken. It's just that-" a dry heave interrupts him mid sentence- "It's just that I just found a really thick, long black hair in my Hoagie. It was fuggin' disgusting." With that, Janikowski dashes away from the embankment, away from Brady, and away from the rotting tortured body of Heather Harris with his hands pressed tightly over his mouth.

Brady closes his notebook and starts to walk back towards his car. He can still hear the sickening retching sounds of Officer Janikowski, now coming from behind a police cruiser. Behind him, Detective Emeonye is carefully placing the newly discovered finger into an evidence bag. A wry smile adorns her face.

Tripp Durden is from a small town just North of Atlanta. He currently works at a private school in an admin position while coaching football and lacrosse. His goal is to one day create stories full time. As a writer, he strives to write what comes to mind without judging the ideas or the stories too harshly due to the belief that even a bad story is one worth hearing. "A Loss Of Appetite" was inspired by the stories told by his family members who work as first responders.

GORMLEY / THE ARCHITECT / UNTITLED
MARC CARVER

GORMLEY

As I drive up the road
I see a man on a flat roof
he is like one of those Gormley statues.
He is perfectly still
as he looks out into the distance he does not move at all
could almost be dead
it is like he is looking at this land for the first time
like
it never existed before he got up on that roof
and now he doesn't want to come down
so
he is turned to stone
When I drive past later
I will see if he is still there looking for something that he will never
find.

THE ARCHITECT

There is no feeling
like the feeling you get when you wake up at four in the morning
and know you are the only one alive

the deadness
the stillness
you could almost be dead yourself and not know it.
You start to think with a clarity that has alluded you your whole life
no doubts
nothing to hold you back
and suddenly you want to build
brick after brick those words that speak out from the darkness
tell stories that no one will ever hear
but they shout out of the silence like alarm bells warn the sailors of
the rocks that lurk underneath.
So you piece them together
and you know you are making something you don't know or need to
know what it is you only find out when you finish
then you can stand back and see what it is
as if you knew before you started
then you look and know and see what it is
and for once you know what it is

UNTITLED

I think about whether I should put this out into the world
just one more just one more.
Even if I only send it to one person
just one more just one more.
So people can see that I am an artist, I can create still
just one more just one more
but I have given up on the world
just one more just one more.
The stillness that gives me this bed is the only thing I want
Just one more just one more

So if I hit send or not the chances are the world will not see it
but no one will lose much sleep for me
so for the last time the very last time one more time

Marc Carver has published ten collections of poetry but to him the most important thing is to get an email from someone he does not know that says they enjoy his work.

THE MAN WALKS THE ART DISTRICT
EDWARD VIDAURRE

There's a man that walks my neighborhood.

He wears slacks and a polo shirt, he never seems to sweat in any season. He walks and waves hello to all. The skeletons that peek through the shadows, the tiresome barking chihuahua behind the chain link fence, the yellow abandoned home, the widow, the abused, the downtrodden, the newlyweds, the divorcée, the unplanned children crying behind the stained curtain at the window, he waves hello to all. Today it's 103 degree Fahrenheit, he stopped to say hello and all I saw were my hibiscus reflecting in his eyes, three blocks of anguish, and the secret of what lies in the house with the red door, my door.

Edward Vidaurre is the 2018-2019 McAllen, Texas Poet Laureate and author of five collections of poetry. Editor of Called To Rise: Rio Grande Valley Youth Anthology (McAllen Poet Laureate Anthology Series Volume I) Twenty: Poems in Memoriam, and founder of Pasta, Poetry & Vino - a reading series in the Rio Grande Valley. Vidaurre is the editor/publisher for FlowerSong Books an indie press out of south Texas. He resides in McAllen, Texas with his wife and daughter. He writes from the front lines of the Mexican-American borderlands.

GRANDMOTHER MOUNTAIN
MARTHA MCCOLLOUGH

follow water
downhill

they say
follow game trails

to dry moss, lichen
dry pine needles
dry pith of stars

admit: you have
complained (a lot)
about your bones

that might be it
the reason
anyway they left

(you don't
remember the wolves
smiling quite
so red)

left you
to be queen of
this mountain where

grandmothers look
up at the stars

mountain where
grandmothers are
quite old

a softwood peak
that flames
can hungrily climb

You don't
remember
saying
You go on,
I can't make it
or
Leave me, go,
it's your only hope

but you
are quite old
after all, forgetful

lashed together with
stringy roots, last
of the dry pith

queen
of cottongrass
cattails
Big Dipper

queen
of elderberry
shoots

too old to follow
water downhill

say you don't
remember

stay here
eating deep forest

your bones ache
the wolves howl

Martha McCollough is a writer and visual artist who lives in Chelsea, Massachusetts. She has an MFA in painting from Pratt Institute. Her poems are forthcoming or have appeared in Tampa Review. The Baffler, Crab Creek Review, and Salamander, among others. Her videopoems have appeared in Triquarterly, Datableed, and Atticus Review.

"Grandmother Mountain" was previously published by Blue Lyra Press (http://bluelyrareview.com/blue-lyra-press/)

RIVA RUN
SARAH SAXTON STRASSBERG

"Hulk versus Iron Man."

"Hulk."

"Wrong."

"What?"

"Iron Man can literally fly circles around Hulk. Plus, he has JARVIS. All Hulk can do is throw rocks around."

"Hulk could throw a rock at Iron Man. It could disable his rockets," James said, fiddling with the blue and lime green paracord bracelet that hung loosely around his wrist.

"You really think Tony Stark would let himself get squashed by a giant rock?" Willie raised his eyebrows.

"Fine. Iron Man wins." James flipped over and let his arm dangle off of the tree house platform. Below, the rope ladder twisted in the breeze, the wooden rungs creaking lightly. "My turn. Captain America versus Spider-Man."

Willie scoffed. "Are you kidding? Spider-Man would web up Cap and his shield in no time. Not even Super-Soldier Serum can beat Peter Parker's webbing. Black Widow or Scarlet Witch?"

"I don't know." James swung his arm back and forth, back and forth from the platform.

"Oh, come on," Willie said. "You always know. Don't be a dweeb."

James turned his head and looked down at his hand, clenching and unclenching in midair. "I'm not a dweeb."

"What is wrong with you today?" Willie brushed his blond hair away from his forehead, exposing the crisscross of white and red ravines and ridges that stretched across the left side of his face.

"Nothing."

Willie crawled over to James and sat cross-legged next to him. "Quicksilver or Thor?"

"I don't know," James repeated.

"Thor. His hammer beats everything, even Quicksilver's speed. Plus, immortality." Willie mimicked an uppercut punch.

"I should be getting home," James said. "My mom said dinner's at six." He kneeled and brushed himself off before stepping down onto the highest rung of the rope ladder.

"I want to stay here," Willie said.

"I gotta go," James said. He started down the ladder, descending two rungs at a time, hands and feet flying. The moss and mud on the forest floor gave way slightly to his sandals. "You coming?" he called up to Willie.

Willie's tousled head appeared at the edge of the platform. "I'll be down later."

"Okay. See you tomorrow."

Willie waved with his good arm. "See you later!"

James picked up Willie's crutch from the mud and propped it against the massive sycamore tree. The silvery metal gleamed dully against the mossy bark.

The earthy smell of late summer filled James' nostrils, and the light streaming through the trees was more golden than green. Something rustled through the undergrowth and vanished. On the ground, the heat and humidity were almost stifling, though the occasional breeze sent murmurs of movement through the leaves.

He took off his sandals and ran home, his shoes swinging from his grasp the entire way.

After he vaulted the garden gate with six inches to spare, he rinsed his muddy feet in the sprinkler, watching the brown rivulets run down his toes and drip from his heels. Specks of dirt still stubbornly remained under his toenails, strips of black stark against the pink quick. When he put his sandals back on, the insoles squelched slightly.

"James! Where have you been? It's almost six-thirty!" Mrs. Giornio shouted from the open kitchen window, wiping her hands on her cooking apron. An apple pie was cooling on the windowsill.

"Sorry, Mom," James said. "I lost track of time. I was at the treehouse with Willie."

Mrs. Giornio gave a stiff nod. "Oh. I see. Dinner's on the table, honey."

James scurried through the screen door on the porch, washed his hands, and sat at the table with the rest of his family.

"Where on earth were you?" Claire whispered, picking at her red nail polish. Small chips broke off and scattered into the lap of her jeans.

"Treehouse," James said.

"Hmm," Claire said and began heaping mashed potatoes onto her plate. "Last time I checked, that treehouse wasn't interesting enough to hang out there for hours alone."

"You haven't been up there in four years. And I wasn't alone," James said. "I was with Willie. Like always."

Mr. Giornio cleared his throat. "I can't believe school starts Tuesday. This summer has flown by."

"Ugh," Claire said. "Good luck with not dying, James. Millwood is super fun."

"Claire." Mr. Giornio gave her a stern look over his glasses. "Be nice."

"Sorry." Claire suddenly became very interested in her potatoes and corn.

"At least I'll have Willie," James said. "I can't imagine going to school without him."

Mrs. Giorno leaned over and patted James on the shoulder. "Of course, dear. You will always have Willie."

"What classes are you taking again, James?" Mr. Giorno asked. "It's been so long since registration that I've forgotten."

James toyed with his potatoes, raking his fork in swirls to form a zen garden that smelled of garlic. "Just the usual. Math, science, history, English, P.E., music. Same old, same old."

"But you're going to junior high!" Mrs. Giornio said. "It's going to be a big change. Isn't that right, Claire?"

Claire shrugged. "I guess. Not compared to some things."

"Claire!" Mrs. Giornio snapped.

James dropped his fork and knife. The clatter of silver on ceramic was deafening. "You're talking about Willie, aren't you?" he asked, his tone even but tinged with rage. "Just because he's all banged up now doesn't mean he isn't a person. It doesn't mean he isn't still my friend."

"You're right, James," Mr. Giornio finally said.

They finished dinner in silence, the only sounds the scraping of utensils and the muffled murmuring of the TV in the living room. Outside, the natural light was fading into greyish-gold dusk, signaling the rapid shortening of autumn days. A sparrow settled on a branch of the dogwood tree next to the window and chirped. James tapped the window with his knuckle, and the sparrow took off, looping around the backyard once before disappearing into the trees. He jumped at the sight of a small, skinny blond boy leaning on a crutch in the middle of the yard.

"Willie's here," James said, leaping up and slamming the screen door open. He dodged the sprinkler and stopped a few feet in front of Willie. "What are you doing? Your parents are gonna flip!"

Willie adjusted his crutch. "I don't want to go home. It's like they don't even see me anymore. They think I'm ugly."

"I see you," James said. "And I don't think you're ugly. You've got battle scars, like Nick Fury. It's cool."

"The kids at school won't think so."

"I think it's cool."

Willie shook his head. "Look at your sister. She's mean. They're all mean."

"The kids in our class sent flowers and cards after the accident, remember? That wasn't mean."

"Things are going to be different. Junior high isn't the same."

"Want to sleep over tonight? If your family doesn't mind?"

"They won't mind."

"You sure?"

"Yeah."

James looked back at the kitchen window, where the pie was still sitting. "We just finished dinner, but there's probably going to be dessert if you want it."

"I'm not really hungry. Can we ride?"

"Can you?"

Willie shrugged. "Well enough."

"You can borrow Claire's bike if you want. She won't mind too much," James said. "I can lower the seat for you. Gimme one second." He ran back up to the screen door and shouted into the kitchen. "I'm going on a ride with Willie, Mom."

Mrs. Giornio looked up from washing the dishes. "It's getting dark, James. Why don't you send Willie home and stay here?"

"Willie wants to go for a ride."

"Stay here, James. It'll be dark, and it's not safe."

Willie nudged James in the ribs with his elbow. "Come on. It'll be fun. Don't be a dweeb."

Being careful to avoid the indentation in Willie's side, James returned the gesture. "I'm not a dweeb. I'll go."

"James?" Mrs. Giornio called.

"Tell her you're saying bye to me," Willie whispered.

James hesitated. "I'll get in trouble."

Willie scoffed. "So what? That's never bugged you before."

"Fine," James said after a pause. "Mom, I'm saying goodbye to Willie. I'll be there in a little bit." He turned to Willie. "If I get in trouble, I'm going to kick your butt!"

Willie stuck his tongue out. "Worth it! Let's go."

The boys tiptoed to the garage, and James heaved the door open. He flicked the light switch on the wall, and the single light flickered to life, illuminating Mr. Giornio's compact car, trash and recycling cans, and four bikes suspended from a rack. James turned to Willie, and his breath caught in his throat for a split second.

In the warm half-light, the damages of Willie's body were all too evident–the hunched spine, the gashes on his face, the uneven spiderwebs snaking across his skin. His shirt, although loose, could not hide the odd twist of his back and the unevenness of his shoulders, and a maze of scars cast a crisscross of shadows on his distorted arm. Beside the crutch, his knee resembled that of a four-legged creature, bent inwards and backwards and lacking frontal definition. His athletic shorts hid the upper portion of his leg, but the way he distributed his weight suggested a mangled thigh and hip.

"Did it hurt?" James asked quietly.

Willie gave a sharp, snorting laugh. "I don't know what hurt worse, the car or the doctors trying to fix me."

"Are you sure you want to ride? We can play Avengers Assemble instead."

"What's that thing people say? Something about getting back on a horse?"

"I think it's 'If you fall off a horse, get right back on it.'"

Willie nodded. "That's it." He shifted to the side with a slight groan, then looked up at James. "Don't look at me like that."

"What?"

"You're looking at me the way all the other kids are gonna look at me. Like I'm a freak. Like there's something wrong with me."

James raised his forearms in defense. "You're not a freak. I never said there was anything wrong with you. What do you want me to do, not look at you?"

"That's what everyone else is doing, so no. They're all looking right through me like I'm not even there. Just treat me like normal, okay?"

"Nothing about this–" James gestured to Willie's scarred limbs and torso. "Nothing about this is normal, Willie. Things are different now. I'm trying."

"Try harder," Willie said, his voice edged with an icy shakiness. "Get the bikes down."

James braced the back wheel of Claire's bike with one hand as he lifted the frame up and out of the supportive hook. He staggered a little under the bulky weight before setting it down and adjusting the seat height. "When was the last time you rode?" he asked as he lifted his mountain bike from the rack.

"I tried my bike a week or two ago. I rode up and down the street a few times."

"And?"

The crutch creaked as Willie shrugged. "It was fine. Didn't hurt as much as I thought it was going to. Wasn't as fun as I thought it was going to be."

"So to the cul-de-sac and back tonight?"

"I want to go to Thornton."

James drew back. "Are you sure? That's five miles there and back, plus hills. And we'd have to cross..."

"Riva Run? I know. Getting back on the horse, remember?"

"I don't know if this is a good idea," James said. "For you or me. And it's getting dark. Cars won't be able to see us."

Willie bent down and pinched the front tire of Claire's bike between his thumb and index finger to test the air pressure. "Now you're starting to sound like your mom. Come on. It'll be fun."

"Another accident like that would kill you."

"I'm not scared."

James kicked at the back tire of his bike. "So you're not scared of being hit by a car again, but you are scared of the kids at school? What kind of messed-up logic is that? What the hell is wrong with you?"

"Screw you," Willie said.

Before James could answer, Willie swung one leg over the seat of Claire's bike and tossed his crutch to the side, sweeping the ground with his good foot a few times to gain speed before pedaling up the driveway. The bike wobbled slightly as he fought to keep his body upright and balanced.

"Hey, wait up!" James called, mounting his bike and chasing after Willie. "I'm sorry! I didn't mean it!"

Willie refused to respond. He was riding much faster than James expected, and James was out of breath before they had even reached the end of the road. As Willie rode under the streetlights, the red reflective square on the back of the bike glimmered, farther and farther ahead of James with each passing minute. Several times, James thought he had lost him but then managed to catch sight of the little red square somewhere down the road. The headlights of the occasional car passing by revealed Willie's silhouette, crooked and hunched over the handlebars while he pedaled furiously with his good leg, letting the injured one go through the motions loosely.

Sweat trickled down James's neck and back, surprisingly cold against the sticky humidity of the late August night, and the wind whipped his hair back from his face. His lungs and calves burned from the exertion, and a stitch in his side was stabbing relentlessly with every breath. He swerved at the last second to avoid running over a dead squirrel in the road, and his left foot slipped from the pedal. The coated plastic slammed against his exposed heel, ripping the skin away in one wrenching motion. He let out a shallow cry but ignored the pain, steadying the bike and pedaling even faster. The streetlights lining the way were now fewer and farther between, and the sky was growing darker. He was practically riding blind.

"Willie!" he screamed into the wind, to no response. He coasted to a halt at the bottom of a hill under a light and examined his heel. The back of his sandal was already stained deep red, and an inch of upper layer of skin was gone. "Ow," he hissed as he gently prodded the area to assess the damage.

"Are you okay?" Willie asked from behind James, making him jump.

James nodded. "It's just a scratch. Where were you? I couldn't see you anywhere."

Willie shifted his weight. "I circled back around."

"I'm sorry. About earlier. I didn't mean it."

"Follow me," Willie said, turning Claire's bike away. He twisted his scarred mouth into a half-smile.

James averted his eyes and pretended to re-examine the wound in his heel. The bleeding had not slowed at all. When he looked up, Willie was already at the top of the hill, stopped perpendicular to the road and bracing the bike with his good leg. Grunting as he pushed off the ground with his injured foot, James began to follow Willie. As soon as he got within fifteen feet, Willie took off, but at a significantly slower pace this time. James had little trouble keeping up with him as they crested hill after hill along the winding road.

It was only when he rounded the bend and saw the sea of headlights, like hordes of anglerfish ripping through midnight zone waters, that he realized where they were. He slowed to a stop next to Willie, who was staring hungrily at the cars slashing back and forth on the highway. The lights illuminated his ruined face and the desire in his eyes.

"I told you this was a bad idea," James said. "We shouldn't be here."

Willie laughed, but there was something cold in his voice. "Cross it. I dare you."

"No."

"I double dare you."

"No." James wiped sweat out of his eyes. "Stop."

"It's a double dare. You have to do it. I'll be right behind you."

"Why are you doing this?"

"Back on the horse. I told you."

James shook his head. "No. No. We'll both die."

"I'll go first, then." Willie started toward the highway, and James reached out and yanked him back by the arm. Claire's bike clattered to the ground, and Willie fell onto his injured side. For a moment, he lay completely still, then he writhed onto all fours, his back arched with either pain or rage.

"Help me up," Willie growled.

"Not if you're just going to kill yourself," James said. He let his bike fall and took a few steps backward. "Stop. You–you can't die."

Willie forced his body into a kneeling position. His injured knee was bent at an impossible angle. "Help me up," he repeated through gritted teeth. "Something bad happens, you have to deal with it. You have to deal with it somehow."

"What are you talking about?" James hissed. "You're not making any sense."

"You just don't get it, do you?" Willie asked. He let out a sharp laugh that turned into a coughing fit and knocked him back onto his hands and knees.

"Get what? Willie, what the hell?"

"Look," Willie said, raising a single, shaking finger and pointing toward the road.

James threw up his hands. "What do you want?"

"Just go look! Get closer."

"No! No. I'm not going anywhere near that road."

Willie braced himself against Claire's fallen bike and forced his body into an upright position. "You have to see. You'll understand then." He limped closer to the highway and beckoned for James to follow him.

"You're sick!"

Willie stopped and let out a deep breath. "You're right," he said. "I am sick. I'm worse than sick. But you're right there with me. You know it."

"What?" James shielded his eyes from the glare as a car with its high-beams on passed.

He inched toward Willie until they were nearly side by side, only a few feet from the road, and held out his hand. "We're going home. Come on."

"I wish," Willie said quietly. He looked over at the short wall that separated the forest from the highway.

James traced Willie's gaze to a dark mass that lay at the base of the wall. Another car whooshed by them, lighting up the wooden cross and fresh flowers and whipping the ribbons into a frenzy.

"No," James whispered. "No, no, no." He stumbled to the memorial and traced the letters engraved on the cross, the flashing of the headlights hypnotic and the smell of lilies and gasoline intoxicating.

In Loving Memory
William Roger Clements
October 27, 2006 – April 4, 2018

When James looked up, only the vast darkness of the hills met him. He stumbled to his feet and clambered back along the path, away from Riva Run. When he pressed the back of his trembling hand against his cheek, he felt the streams running down his face and tasted the salty sweetness as they invaded his chapped lips. He blinked a few times and wiped them all away, though his eyelashes remained heavy with stray droplets.

Claire's bike lay sprawled against the incline of the road next to his own, the front tire just barely spinning and the frame twisted at a bizarre angle, like a bird shot from the sky. James pulled both bicycles upright in a single mechanical movement, sheltering the handlebars of each on either side of his ribcage. He did not look back as he walked the bikes home over the winding hills and under the stark, angelic fluorescence of the streetlights.

Sarah Saxton Strassberg is the author of The Queen Anne Society, a mystery-adventure novel about Blackbeard's lost treasure. She is currently studying Biology and Medicine, Health, & Society at Vanderbilt University in Nashville. In her spare time, she enjoys drawing, dancing, reading, and petting as many dogs as humanly possible.

THE REUNION OF HER BONES
EG TED DAVIS

And they buried her bones
in two different geographical locations;
one part upon a humidity filled tropical island,
the home of her youth,
the other in a place of extreme summer's
desert heat and harsh winter freezes-
an upper desert overgrown with sagebrush-
a place of her widower's dreams.

And over the years,
the anniversaries of her death pass...

until there comes a springtime-
where warmth begins to
extend its charm and
new growth shoots appear-

only to become burned by
the expansion of a Red Giant
(the once life giving star),
the sign of the end times,
for this world has finally
aged out and arrived
to its own conclusion,
just as all life forms have
since the beginning of time.

and her bones cry out...

Let us reunite

EG Ted Davis is a poet living in Boise ID with work that has, or will, appear in various online literary journals both here in the US and in the UK..

FLOATING
SUNSET COMBS

I am going to a family event, another Christmas or Thanksgiving or Easter get-together. There is no sign of snow, yet no sign of heat. The temperature is nonexistent. I walk up to my grandparent's green porch, through the world with no air, and through the glass door. My family is in a tight group in the living room, standing and talking amongst paisley chairs and pillows. And in the middle, my small, brown-eyed aunt is staring at me, alive even though we buried her months ago. She always comes to me in dreams as her old self. Not the dying woman, not the stuffed woman in a coffin. As she died, her skin became pale, her body thin, her face sunken, skeletal. In her coffin, her eyes were too obviously sewn, her skin puffy from slow, painful death, her body just skin and bones, floating in her fancy green funeral suit with brass buttons. Her float into death and out of our lives. Smooth on the water, slow. But inside, she suffered a big ocean storm, waves crashing, salt water in her eyes, in her mouth. Struggle.

I walk into my grandparent's living room and my aunt is alive, the old version of herself, and she is staring right at me. This is when someone tells me I have gone to a family event in the past. Oh, of course, I've been invited to the Christmas or Thanksgiving or Easter get-together of 2017. I must have forgotten. Whoever tells me this, I cannot see, but they make sure to give me a warning in hushed tones: "Do not tell her she is going to die." And they leave me with her, my dead aunt, though alive, and her sons who are mourning her when I am not asleep. Her youngest son stares at her, tears in his eyes. He cannot say anything, only stare. There she is, no longer floating. I do the same thing as him, unable to think of conversation topics to share with a ghost. She looks at me expectantly, calling me my nickname only she called me, waiting for me to tell her about school. But I cannot speak, only stare.

She becomes angry with me and starts yelling. And I cannot tell her she will be dead soon. I cannot tell her this is the last time she will see me and recognize me. I cannot tell her the loss her son beside me will suffer. She screams at me, this tiny, frail woman, until she becomes big and raging and I am riddled with guilt. She screams and screams at me for not taking care of my grandmother, says I'm not doing enough. And I cannot tell her that she will die soon. I cannot tell her that she will not live to see her granddaughters' first birthday. I cannot tell her that her mother will be lost, lost, floating without her and there will be nothing I can do for my grandmother, just like there was nothing I could do for my aunt.

I go back to the present and my aunt is dead again. In the dream, my grandmother has gone and floated beside her, died from loneliness and grief. My grandmother's husband, losing himself to dementia, is blaming me and only me. I know he will come for rabid revenge. I push my boyfriend into a nonexistent bunker in the nonexistent basement of my grandmother's house. I am telling him, "We need to hurry," because it won't be long before I float with my aunt and grandmother. We hide in the bunker, all blank and dark, an imagined memory. But I fear the lock on the bunker door isn't enough to save us. I tell my boyfriend, "Stay here where it's safe," and I emerge from the bunker in a big, pink Easter Bunny costume, cheeks hard and round, whiskers long and white and scratchy. I run around, trying to lock all the doors to keep my grandmother's husband out, feeling the weight of the bunny costume pulling me down.

I peer out the window, checking for threats, and notice my car is still parked on the road in front of my grandparent's house. That I have completely given us away. I run outside, where the sky has ceased to exist, and I try to get to my car to park it in the garage, to protect us. I will make it seem like no one is home. But just as I am about to pass the white mailbox and reach my car, I am stopped by a mound of plastic Easter eggs, on the bushes and in the grass, all the candy spilling out. I pick one up, a pink one I think, and it looks so perfectly real. Nothing like a dream. The nonexistent sun is shining through the cheap plastic at the top, an unreliable snap leaves it hanging open, three holes in the bottom of the egg are felt by the fleshy skin on my fingers.

My grandmother's husband, my step-grandpa, my grandfather used to hide the Easter eggs every year. Twenty bucks in only one of the eggs for someone to find, but my grandmother would always tell my grandfather to point discreetly at where he had hidden it, so I was always the one who got the prize. I would stick my money in my basket, on top of countless pieces of chocolate and colored confetti, a treasure in those days. Even though I know my boyfriend and I will be found if I leave my car outside and even though I know being found means being killed, I cannot help myself when I see those eggs in the yard. I have no choice, not really, but to collect them, to stoop and pull them all against my furry chest, hurriedly scraping candy and plastic shells from grass blades into my arms, running back to my grandparent's house to keep them safe with me and my boyfriend who is awaiting my return in the bunker.

I don't realize until later that I have fallen for my grandfather's trap. I don't realize until later that while I was on my hands and knees, collecting his placed Easter eggs, I had felt eyes watching me from the surrounding trees. That I had felt something that I could not escape floating towards me.

Sunset is a senior at Earlham College, majoring in English and minoring in Creative Writing. Her work has also been published in The Crucible at Earlham College and The Paragon Press: Echo, an online Nonfiction journal.

SPACE BONES
MARIE HOWALT

Day 001

I was asked to keep a diary and send it down. A personal one in addition to the log we keep aboard the station. I think they told all five of us to do it. It has something to do with the injections.

We all signed up for experimental treatment, and it is the first time anyone tests the effect in low gravity for a longer period of time. But you know that. Or, I imagine that you do. I imagine you're a doctor or research assistant back on Earth receiving these updates.

Yesterday's launch went smoothly. The trip to the station went like any other, and docking went fine as well. It was Moreno's first time leaving Earth and doctor Ortega's too, I think, but the rest of us have been in orbit before. For me, it's the fourth time, but I've never been away for more than a month. The first time, in other words, that I'm going to be in danger of the osteoporosis that comes with prolonged weightlessness.

Rogers brags about having to piss out kidney stones the size of table tennis balls (I'm no doctor, but I'm pretty sure that's not even possible) multiple times due to insane amounts of calcium in the blood. Boyd doesn't brag or complain, but the first time I saw him, I couldn't believe they would send him back up. I guess the whole point of it is to see if the damages to his lower body can be reversed or at least stopped with the treatments.

Day 007

We had our first post-launch injections today. According to Rogers, it was an osteo-blast! (I bet you science geeks appreciate that one.) Doctor Ortega took a lot of tests too that will probably be in her report, but from what I understood, everything is looking good. I don't feel any side effects apart from being more thirsty than usually. The doctor says this is normal, and that we should all make absolutely sure to stay hydrated. It will help our bodies when the bone structure changes so we can better withstand the problems of being in zero G.

Day 012

Like I said yesterday, it was Derek's birthday. We drank to him and Rogers insisted we should sing. Derek Moreno, the jolly good fellow in question, was blushing furiously. He's the youngest of us, and I think he may have a thing for Rogers. Honestly, I can't hold that against him.

She's got a potty mouth, but she has a beautiful smile and a great body. Should I delete that last bit?

No, you know what? This is supposed to be a personal account, so that's what you're going to get.

Besides, Rogers' body is relevant since we are looking for changes. So far, I can report that we still look and feel normal. Rogers tried to convince us that since the injections contain DNA from animals with hydrostatic skeletons, we will probably grow fins. I'm pretty sure fish don't have hydrostatic skeletons. It did occur to me, though, that maybe being injected with animal DNA isn't something I should have agreed to as a vegan. I don't know. It's not the same as eating them or drinking their milk, but still.

Day 015

Boyd had to put an EVA suit and go outside today to do some repairs on the station after the impacts we registered yesterday. Even tiny rocks hurtling through the vacuum of space can do damage, and no one wants to wait until it's too late.

Now, there are really two Boyds. Boyd on Earth, and Boyd in zero G. I noticed this immediately after we arrived. He has elegance to him out here. He looks like he belongs, if that makes any sense. Anyway, that's why we all thought doing the repairs would be a piece of cake for him. You have the official reports, so you know how the rope snagged and he broke his leg. What you probably don't know is how he shrugged it off, saying, "Who needs legs out here anyway?"

He's a tough old man.

Day 018

Remember Boyd's broken leg? Well, it's not broken anymore. Ortega examined it this morning after he said it didn't hurt at all. We were all surprised, but the doctor said bone regeneration is a side effect of the injections. I don't think she had expected the fracture to heal that fast, though. Rogers suggested breaking a few bones on each of us to see what happens, but Ortega told her there will be none of that. There are no other visible changes to Boyd's physique.

We are all feeling fine, though Rogers keeps talking about steaks and red meat. Usually that kind of thing grosses me out, but for once, I am not repulsed by the idea. I'm even starting to miss meat myself. I guess I'm just growing immune to her bullshit.

Day 020

Tomorrow is injection day. I am very thirsty. I think the others are too. I see Derek sucking at a water pack at least as often as I do. But we all go about our respective work on the station, follow our assigned sleep cycles, and so on. It's a harmless side effect, so it's fine.

Day 024

I have no idea how it happened. There are safety procedures for everything Derek does in that lab of his. I know he is working with high energy sources, but something like that should not be able to happen!

The remaining stump had been cauterized by the beam, thankfully, or he would have bled out before Boyd and I even found him. As it was, there were only small orbs of blood drifting through the room. Derek was in shock, poor kid. At first, he just kept repeating something about teeth that made no sense. After the drugs kicked in, he said he had no memory of the accident.

Strangely, the footage of his lab was corrupt. And ... Shit, I don't know how to say this. I saw the others look at it too, like they were trying to solve an equation. I swear it looked like there was less.

Less of the severed arm than there should be. Like it would be too short if put back on. It sounds crazy. I know.

Day 025

It's growing back.

One thing is a fractured bone mending really fast, but an arm growing back? I think they could have at least mentioned the possibility to us when we agreed to take part in this experiment! I mean, it's not a bad thing. It's great. Derek will be back to how he was in a few days at this rate, but... It's just freaky. There, I said it. It's freaky.

I asked Ortega which animals exactly the DNA in the injections came from to make sense of all this. She told me it's a subspecies of Hirudinea. I had to look that up. Not exactly what I had expected. I guess it's too late to be reading the fine print and having second thoughts. And they did test the treatments before starting us on them.

Day 027

You don't want to spill things in zero G. Not drinks, and not blood. I did not lose an arm or anything remotely as serious as that, and I wouldn't normally even mention such a small cut, but I'm doing it for two reasons. First of all, it healed after a few hours. I don't mean it stopped bleeding then. I mean healed as in you can't tell it was ever there.

The other reason is the others' reactions to it. Rogers was next to me, and the moment it happened, she grabbed my wrist and pulled my hand to her. She closed her lips around my bleeding finger before I could protest. Like I said, rogue liquids in an environment like this are not a good idea, so I would have put my finger in my own mouth until I could get to a bandage. She probably just wanted to help. But she was ... She was sucking. Hard. I don't know if it was supposed to be flirting or what, but I could feel her teeth, and she made this little moan. I had to push her away and tell her I got it, and she gave me this odd stare before licking my blood off her lips. When I turned around, Boyd and Derek were floating behind us, staring. Smiling.

Day 028

Today was supposed to be injection day. I talked to Ortega about it while she was doing her routine checkup of me. She asked me if I had noticed any changes, and I told her about my concerns. Not just the thirst or the fact that I'm starting to think I need more than regular rations and huge amounts of water. I told her I feel there are side effects to the treatment that none of us were prepared for. Not only healing, but the other things too.

Ortega said she has been in contact with Earth and they can't see any reason to stop now when the injections are clearly having an effect. I asked her what would happen if some of us want to quit.

"Do you want to stop?" she asked me.

I nodded. I don't want to be a quitter. I don't want to be a coward, but there is such a thing as common sense.

The doctor looked me in the eyes and told me she wouldn't force anyone to keep taking the injections. She lowered her voice as if someone might overhear us, and as if that would be bad, and said, "I stopped a week ago."

Day 036

I was trying to convince myself that it was okay to stop the injections. That it might even be interesting for you guys to compare us after the experiment ends. I was trying to convince myself that all the concerns I have written about over the past few days are just psychological. That I'm feeling like a traitor for quitting the treatments and not telling anyone besides the doctor about it.

But the way the others look at me... The way they move and act... It's like they know. It's like they are planning something. I know it sounds paranoid. But it isn't. I'll go talk to doctor Ortega about it. I haven't seen her since yesterday.

Day 036, Addition

Ortega is dead. I am in her cabin now. There isn't any blood. At all, I mean. She has small wounds on her wrists and neck, but they are not bleeding. Not because of coagulation. I don't know how to say it, but she looks wrong. Too flat, somehow. I think she has been drained. Of blood, I mean. Of liquid. The wounds look like something bit her. Or someone. I have been sitting here for two hours now, waiting to see if she will come back. Regenerate like Boyd and Derek, but I don't think she will. Maybe it's because she stopped the injections. Maybe it's because nobody comes back from the dead. Shit. I don't know what to do. I need to get through to Earth. This diary is only being sent at intervals along with the reports. I need to talk to someone now.

Day 036, Addition

Communications are out. Boyd says he might have missed some damage when he was outside the station, but I don't believe him. I don't believe any of them. I don't know who killed Ortega, but I'm staying out of their way as much as I can, and I'm watching my back.

A shuttle is scheduled to arrive in three months, but they have to send someone before that, right? If they don't hear anything from the station, Earth has to send someone to see what is going on. Right?

Day 042

I don't know why I keep writing when I can't send these entries anyway. Maybe it's stupid, but I feel better doing it. And when someone comes to pick us up, my diary will help me remember exactly what happened and when.

It's injection day again. Since we don't have a doctor anymore, Rogers said we should do it ourselves. She was showing her teeth in a smile that looked like a sneer when she handed me a syringe. I pretended I was going to use it. I fear what will happen if I tell her I'm not taking them anymore.

Day 045

I hate the way they move. I hate the way they stare at me. I hate how they squeeze the water packs and suck at them like they want to tear them open.

Rogers sniffed me today. I hadn't heard her slither up behind me until she was breathing on my neck. Her voice was too dry and husky as she asked me if I am taking my injections. I said that of course I am. Then she frowned and told me I smell differently. She licked her lips and told me I smell delicious. Normally, I would have written it off as flirting, but there is nothing normal about all this.

Day 046

They were fighting today. We have been using more water than the station is able to recycle, and I think Derek was hoarding water packs for himself. I heard them shouting, if that's even the word for the sounds they made. When I peeked around the corner, I saw them scrabbling for the packs, swatting at each other. Rogers managed to snatch one and ripped it open with her teeth as I watched. Boyd and Derek both tried to take it. Seeing them push off from the wall to hurl themselves at her, seeing her claw at Boyd's face, seeing Derek try to catch the escaping droplets of blood and water alike and licking at his hands... It's not right.

I think I will have to do something. I don't know what. I just know I don't want to end up
like Ortega.

Day 047

They know I'm not taking the injections. Boyd told me I'm not one of them. That's the most sensible thing anyone has said on this station for a long time. But not being one of them means more than just being an outsider. It means I am prey. I have to take action. I have to take action now.

I'm not going to wait for them to move first. If you don't hear from me again, they have killed me.

Day 047, Addition

I'm alive.

I'm alive.

Shit. I can hear them through the door. One of them just pounded on it or was thrown against it. All three of them are screaming.

I still don't know how I did it. You can't run through a space station like a building on Earth.

I took the three water packs that were left and started towards Ortega's empty cabin. Rogers saw me and called out to the others. I have never moved so fast in zero G before.

I threw the packs into the cabin, saw them float through the door in slow motion, and tried to flatten myself against the wall. Boyd and Derek went in like dogs after a hunk of meat. But Rogers stopped and stared at me. Her eyes... Her eyes did not look right. She reached out for me. I pushed off from the wall, holding the railing to get momentum and planted both feet in her abdomen. She howled as she sailed towards the others. I hit the button that closes off all sections in the case of emergency. Alarms started blaring. The door slammed shut.

The cabin door is still closed. Every door on the station is. I am trapped in this small section of corridor. I have moved to the far end of it, but I can still hear them. Even over the alarms.

Another body slammed against the door right now. I think they are fighting. I... I have to hope they are. And they are still screaming. I can't make out any words. It's been days since I heard any of them talk. I wonder if they even can at this point.

All I can do now is wait. Wait for the screams to stop.

They say the human body is 60 percent water. Even our bones consist of roughly 30 percent water.

I wonder if that is still true.

I wonder if they are still human.

I hope they are not.

Physically located in Copenhagen, Denmark, Marie Howalt travels to other dimensions by writing about the far future, fantasy worlds or alternate realities and the people in them and would love to take you along for the ride.

You might think skeletons would be easy to avoid if you had a mild phobia of them. That appears not to be the case, however, because Marie keeps being confronted by craniums, femurs, and scapulas at home thanks to a flatmate who enthusiastically collects bones, although said flatmate reassures everybody that most of these are in the closet.

Marie's traditionally published debut novel, We Lost the Sky, was released in 2019 by Spaceboy Books. Its sequel is on the way, but if you get impatient, you can read a couple of serial novels on Marie's Patreon and Inkitt profiles (you can find links on http://www.mhowalt.dk) or say hi on Twitter or Instagram @mhowalt..

BENEATH OUR SKIN
ELLA TOUPIN

The bones beneath our skin will rattle one day, just as those before us do right now.

Beneath our feet they lie in over sized boxes, rattling reminiscently about the lives they once lived.

Those are free of their fleshy confines, unlike ours, which wait patiently for their time to come.

For now they stay diligently beneath our skin, permitting our muscles and tissue to share their space.

One day they will break through the oppressive layers, to rattle lonely beneath others' feet.

There are two-hundred and six bones in the body. Some small as the head of a pin, others big and thick as a tree.

All two-hundred and six of them remain diligently beneath the surface waiting for their time to come.

When our flesh will slide off into nothing, feeding the earth and its inhabitants.

And our bones will rattle six feet under the earth in an oversized box.

Ella is a student working to establish herself in the writing community. She has always found writing to be the purest form of escape, and is drawn to the creation of worlds far away from the chaos of reality.

FACE LIKE VODKA / RUST
ANN CHRISTINE TABAKA

FACE LIKE VODKA

A face like vodka,
a soul like wine,
cocktail of life
drained dry by time

Your cruel departure
left a hole in the universe.
All existence has ceased.

Drowning in intoxicants,
vestiges of sanity gone,
a scent of grapes lingers on.

Birds overhead observe me
grounded supine,
my roots reaching downward
Into the dead earth.

Searching for a reason to exist,
dreams like bourbon,
voice like rum.

You are gone from my life.
Now life becomes a river
of drunk deception.

RUST

Broken-down old cars,
a junkyard's prize away.

Crumbling rust inhaled at dawn,
poison of choice.

Blindness escapes night
in shades of silver gray.

Suspended on a string,
life hangs precariously from above.

I cannot write the green dream,
the blue sky, they are gone from view.

Sins punished by contrition.
Guilt a death sentence.

Now departed from this life,
all is rust, cascading rust, beautiful rust.

Ann Christine Tabaka lives in Delaware. She is a published poet and artist. She loves gardening and cooking. Chris lives with her husband and two cats. Her most recent credits are The Paragon Journal, The Literary Hatchet, Metaworker, Raven Cage Ezine, RavensPerch, Anapest Journal, Mused, Indiana Voice Journal, Halcyon Days Magazine, The Society of Classical Poets, and BSU's Celestial Musings Anthology' Poems Inspired by the Night Sky.'

NO MIDDLE NAME
JACINDA GOH

My birth name was a rib-crushing, hourglass moulding corset
I have always longed to step out of so that my existence will not become
like the bound feet of my great-grandmother:

a pair of stiletto-shaped soles manufactured
with shattered bones, a thing of beauty
bartered with calcium.

My two-part name is sugar and egg whites beaten into a snow-
capped mountain range then put into an oven and expected to rise
but always deflating when removed from heat except for that one time
the browned toque blanche rose out of the baking dish in all the grandeur
of the Hagia Sophia dome, a structure of belligerence, within it held
the clashing armoury of warring religions.

My 'English' name was a dress my mom bought when I was 8
and I found it and tried it on when I was 17 – Jacinda and I thought:
too small, out of style so I tried on Jac, like Jack and the Beanstalk, Jack Sparrow,
familiar names that I used assure some island boys that I was a girl
named Jac.

Pseudo-masculinity was having a male-esque name and thinking it was cool

but novelty is every fickle lover – the expectation to explain
why, the justification of its pronunciation.

The name of my ethnicity is the subtle cocking of a gun
at my ear canal that I never want to hear, a disdainful click
unheard by everyone but me –

for my roots, for my desire to be a part of the White
Western Wonderland I grew up watching on the pixel pieced screen.

It is "baby, I got us" slurring out of your mouth one night, dripping
with the lack of thought like the sap from a gum tree,

the inconsequential words I still hoard in the storeroom of my heart
that felt like tip-toeing at the edge of a white Grecian house on the
cliff-
bounded island, overlooking the Aegean – blood rushing and heart
quivering
as I watched the blue water turn to white foam running into the rocky
shores.

Ten years from where I stand may I still be dancing on the edges of
roofs and cliffs, traversing the dirt roads of the undeveloped on two
wheeled rumbling machines,
past the coconut trees lining the glass-paned water meeting sand,
onto the wooden boardwalk and tower, into the water on epoxy resin
boards,

all with your last name: Nucci – a white chiffon fabric grasping
onto my salt-slicked body, faintly waltzing with the sea breeze.

I have learned to accept brow bones that will never keep the water
from my eyes and Jia, the first sound in the mandarin language,

a straight line, flat and dandy, like the first sixteen years I've used
that name
and Ying, the third sound of the four, a letter V as if to say,

child, you will walk through the valley of the shadow of death
and you will learn that your name is the molten lava
that runs on old land and flows into the cold ocean,
creating new life for years to come.

Jacinda Goh is a recent Sarah Lawrence College graduate. She was born and raised in Singapore, and currently lives in New York City with her pit-bull Hank.

GIANT CACTUS
JACOB KOBINA AYIAH MENSAH

She stood alone by the hearth, trying to cover her half body with the old draper. She took her time not to cause more damage to her skin again, which had many strips hanging from it. The log in the hearth was growing and around this growth in the small kitchen, she was hoping to flower again. She could not see outside again. She stood up for the first time when she entered here after shooting out from that small dig. Once everything was a black seed, dragged, pushed, shoved, along a wet trail by angry and hungry ants in a long chain and suddenly a bird emerged from the mist and swallowed it and later deposited it in its drop of drops. The seed rot in an old cot and grew up as a tree, one of its seed found its way under the porous floor of this kitchen. Here it became a woman. This morning, a visitor came in and took made photographs of her. He had made seeds of her. Many viewers were watching on the television sets this evening. A woman called her saguaro. She said to her son, who is struggling with his mathematics homework, "Big Joe, you see that tree storing water in its trunks and branches for all types of birds, bats and insects, tomorrow we will read about it in the newspapers." The schoolboy looked at the little rain he had already painted in the space and asked himself how to write essay around it. He mentioned its ribs, running lengthwise along both the truck and branches, in his work.

Jacob Kobina Ayiah Mensah is author the of new hybrid works, The Sun of a Solid Torus, Conductor 5, Genus for L Loci and Handlebod y. His individual poems are widely published and recently appearing in Rigorous, Beautiful Cadaver Project Pittsburgh, The Meadow, Juked, North Dakota Quarterly, Cathexis Northwest Press, The Sandy River Review, Strata Magazine, Atlas Poetica, Modern Haiku, etc. He is algebraist and artist and lives in the southern part of Ghana, Spain, and Turtle Mountains, North Dakota.

THREE FACES FROM SPRINGTIME
JOAN MCNERNEY

DEMURE

Soft and sweet buttercup
just starting to blossom.
Her eyes are wide open.

Smiling at blue skies
skipping along avenues in a
sparkling green dress.

KID

As sly as can be,
tricky little imp
playing peek-a-boo.

Connoisseur of mud pies
whistling in the wind.

HIPPIE

Shameless young floozy
elbowing her way out of nowhere
dressed in emerald glad rags.

Sashaying around...sexy sexy
sleeping with lush leaves
and no account wild flowers.

Joan McNerney's poetry has been included in numerous literary zines such as Moonlight Dreamers of Yellow Haze, Seven Circle Press, Dinner with the Muse, Blueline, Halcyon Days and included in Bright Hills Press, Kind of A Hurricane Press and Poppy Road Review anthologies. She has been nominated four times for Best of the Net.

FIVE UNTITLED POEMS
SIMON PERCHIK

*

And though the stars came by
what you hear stays wet
for your hands on the rope
waiting till it's dark –you hang the wash
at night, sure your bones will dry
–by morning you'll fill the tub again
with her dress and stir
till the water turns black
smells from sleeves
and the same shoulders
that were always there
with grass that you add later.

*

You listen the way this stone
senses when its prey
no longer has a pulse
and swallows it whole
though your ears work like that
widen for the embrace
and quiet that afternoon
still wandering the Earth
as rain and those pebbles

a child finds on the beach
-one by one tossed at the sun
or something in between
taking so long to die -what you hear
is losing its breath
is crumbling and in your arms.

*

You can't stop, talk
and far from your mouth
wait for the grass
as the same sound
between your fingers
lowering for lips
-you talk the way rope
takes so long to die
-over and over and over
empty your mouth
filling it with thorns
with shoulders, afternoons.

*

Wild from the cold each splash
is already driftwood
and though you lean into the sink
a single cup anchors on its own
needs to stay in the center
the way every statue is filled

with stones, smells from flowers
and your chest held close, naked
for stars to scatter what's left
and the afternoon –petal by petal
you pour from a night
longing to cover your body
as a single shell, around and around
with nothing inside but the ending
always in the same place.

*

Half iron, half oak, the bed
all night honed on what went wrong
–it's an axe, striking upside down
though you sleep facing north
side by side an empty dress
shaped into bulls and chariots
with your mouth wide apart
louder and louder getting ready
for the slow descent –you sit
on the edge, trying to bleed
to open the sleeves
still reaching out in the dark.

Simon Perchik is an attorney whose poems have appeared in Partisan Review, Forge, Poetry, Osiris, The New Yorker and elsewhere. His most recent collection is The Osiris Poems published by boxofchalk, 2017. For more information including free e-books and his essay "Magic, Illusion and Other Realities" please visit his website at http://www.simonperchik.com.
To view one of his interviews please follow this linkhttps:// www.youtube.com/watch?v=MSK774rtfx8

BONING YOU
KAITLYN ZOLADZ

I caress the smooth curves
Of you porcelain body
Kissing down your spine
Your perfect structure
Lack of organs
Gets me so dry
I love the way
Our bodies clash and clatter
Together. I can feel
Your love
In my bones
Pelvis to pelvis,
A tibular tango
I long to kiss you
Two hundred and six times
One for every part of you
That I love.
Your curvy cranium that I softly caress,
I could fondle your fleshless femur
For the rest of my life.
My lustful love for you,
Like osteosarcoma
Aggressive, spreading
Though your bones.
And, unlike the disease,
There is no treatment
To cure my love for you

Kaitlyn Zoladz is a humor-focused writer of poetry based outside of Philadelphia, who currently possesses the appropriate amounts of all of her appendages. She enjoys writing about odd topics, and poems with weirdly specific subject matter are just her forte. She has not had a work of her's published yet. Currently, she is also working on finishing her first book of poetry, which is a compilation of over eighty poems. She enjoys long walks to the fridge, writing about rotting food, and sculpting octopi in her free time.

MAP OF MY BONES
CATHRYN FOLLMAN

Empty me out,
Disperse the bits and odd ends-the
Important ones-to
Those who will have more
Use for them.
Warm my body
After it has gone cold,
Have the flames replace your arms
And then when I am nothing,
But ash,
Scatter me.
Somewhere tranquil,
In a meadow from a fairytale
With birds and an auburn colored fox.
The flowers will be my comfort
And no one will disturb my sleep.
Or somewhere flashy,
Bursting with energy
And people who never sleep.
It will be nice to be lost for a time
In a city of light.
Or somewhere in the ocean
Full of secret caverns
Where I can hide
And swim with
Aloof creatures lurking
In the depths.

Or somewhere the Earth is dry.
For I will not mind the heat,
Once I am gone.
The sand will feel nice
Between my toes.
Somewhere I will like,
And that you do, too.
Say your goodbyes,
With or without tears.
But please, feel free
To leave a part of yourself behind,
When you let me go.

Cathryn Follman is an aspiring writer from Philadelphia, PA. She is currently obtaining a Bachelor's degree in English and a minor in History, with an emphasis in Creative Writing at Smith College. She has served on the boards for school newspapers and literary magazines. She has been previously published in the HCE Review, Adelaide Literary Magazine and various student literary magazines and newspapers.

FREEDOM'S BRUTAL STING
KATELYN E. RHODES

February 17, 2020, my release date. Today had finally arrived. I've been imprisoned for exactly two years, today. They said I wouldn't last a year, but here I am. It went like any other day. I raised my head off of what felt like a cotton sack filled with Legos. My bare feet burned as they touched the icy concrete floor. As I shoved my socks onto my bare feet and changed my clothes, I thought about how I would feel once I move on. I quickly dismissed those thoughts. I knew I would only feel joy and relief; that's all. I walked to the bathroom to do my morning duties. In the mirror, a woman with bags under her eyes and pure misery displayed upon her face stared back at me. It was breakfast time and I couldn't have felt more indifferent. A pig-faced woman stared at me and snorted, her snout protruded half way over the counter between us. She squealed and ladled a substance that looked as if it came from the compost bin. After breakfast, we took a long, miserable commute back to our cells.

Every day is the same. Monotonous. Soul-sucking. They said two years would be good for me, yet my life has dramatically changed for the worse since the day I set foot in here. There has been nothing but snickering beasts and hairy ogres glaring at me. For what, because I'm different than they are? I've had enough, but I don't dare engage them. I won't risk a longer sentence by making waves. So, business as usual. I stay in my cell until they see fit to free me, I eat and sleep when I'm told to, and I keep my mouth shut.

Perhaps the most disgusting part of being here is how most of the other prisoners are happy. They have become content with this life-style. I can only assume they tell themselves that they love to be miserable. I, for one, could never be happy in a place like this. They feed us, sure. They even pay us for cheap labor, but this is no life to live. They must be lying to themselves. They are all so shifty; it doesn't surprise me. They put on this happy face, probably because the guards are watching. When they think no one is looking, that's when I see the truth. They are just weasels underneath it all. I see how they transform into such deceiving little rodents. Even if no one else can see, I can.

I know I'll be asked once I'm out, "Why were you in there in the first place?" I won't tell them the whole truth. It's none of their business anyhow. When I'm asked such prying questions—and I know I will be—I'll simply say, "I made a very bad decision in my past that I don't plan on repeating." Something of the sort will do the trick. When I'm finally out, I'll be free. Free to give whatever answers I like.

I sat on the floor of my cell, the brutal sting of the concrete crawled up my arms and chilled my bones as I laid my hands, palm-up on the concrete with my arms limp beside me. I remembered this position all too well. In kindergarten, they had us sit "criss-cross applesauce" on the floor for story time. I loved the feeling of the rug against my fingertips. It felt warm and inviting as I traced the printed roads and buildings beneath me, blissfully oblivious to what my teacher was reading. I had better things to think of then. I thought of where I would be if I didn't have to comply to the rules of the adults in charge. I thought of packing my nap sack and heading to a place where rules didn't exist, where no one would laugh at me because I'm a bit odd. At times, I even thought of sneaking into the pantry near the teacher's desk to burgle the cookie jar. Even at that age, I longed to be free.

Freedom has such a powerful meaning to me now. When I was a child, I often thought of freedom as something you earn from adulthood, a right-of-passage. I wasn't entirely incorrect. Freedom comes with age, yes, but it can be taken away at the drop of a hat. Freedom comes with consequences. There will always be rules to cage us in, especially in school and in our jobs. If you break those rules, well, it costs you your freedom. What little freedom the universe grants us is so precious and we all take it for granted. When I am free, I will truly be free. There will be no one left to tell me how to live. Just me and no one else. Some people strive for love, happiness, or wealth, but freedom is all those things and more. Being imprisoned has enlightened me. Nothing shall cost me my precious freedom ever again.

I looked up from my daydream to see a guard pacing in front of my cell. We made eye contact. At least I thought those were his eyes. His protruding forehead casted such a shadow that his face was nearly nonexistent. Suddenly there were two of them. Their black, beady eyes, barely visible, looked at me with suspicion. Their big green fangs glistened in the fluorescent lights that buzzed overhead. Each step they took was loud and muffled slightly by their body hair; it sounded as if they were trudging through snow. These guards were the reason I hated it here. Every day they paced back and forth in front of my cell, assuming I would make some kind of move as they stared at me and snarled. Their visage flickered in and out, showing me brief images of normal men in suits, minding their own business. When outsiders would come and visit, they were able to change their physique into that of friendly employees. It was enough to make a girl go mad, but not me. "Lunch time, Cruikshank," one of them bellowed at me, tossing a metal tray at the floor in front of me. I asked to be served lunch in my cell today and for once, they actually complied. I won't miss their friendly greetings.

Cruikshank. The guards always called me by my last name here. I suppose it is in efforts to keep their authority over us. As if any of us have an interest in being friends with such hairy beasts. Soon they will be a thing of memories, for I will be released at five p.m. today and I am never looking back. I have prepared my things, cleaned out my area, and all that is left is to wait. Having not a single cellmate for these two years has been maddening, but now I am thankful. No one to distract me from my goal. This evening at five o'clock I will finally be free.

I peered through the iron bars in front of me to make out the time on a clock against the wall. It was half-past noon. Already half my day had passed me by and I hadn't spoke a word to anyone. This wasn't out of the ordinary for me. The weasels and I didn't click much.

I'm not ashamed to say I didn't make a single friend here. Friends become allies and alliances are how fights break out. I needed good behavior, if I was going to survive here. Some of the others gave me strange looks and snickered, but I didn't mind much. I know I went about this the right way. If I got too close to any of them, they might try to sabotage my release date or worse, I might do it myself. I can't have that. I'm leaving today even if it kills me.

2:47. A little over two hours left. This is maddening. The clock began to warp and melt like a Salvador Dali painting. Another hour of this and who knows what I'll do? I could hardly hear my thoughts over the ringing in my ears. My breath began to quicken. I can't take this any longer, I thought as I started to panic.

The book, I thought. I'd read my book to pass the time. *To Kill A Mockingbird*, a classic. Arthur picked it out for me on our second date. He took me to his favorite family-owned book store. He couldn't believe I hadn't read it. The utter shock in his voice made me laugh, but once I read the book, that's when I knew he was the one. It's my favorite now; I could read it forever. It still smells like him after all these years. Maybe, I am just hoping I still remember what he smells like. No, it smells like him, I know it does, I convinced myself.

3:52. I am losing my mind. I can't read this book. I can't sit here like everything is fine, like in an hour I'm not getting back what I rightfully deserve. I've had it. I'm getting out of here.

I got up and walked to those iron bars that have held me captive for two years. With all my strength, I commanded them to open. With one small tug, they did just that. I peeked my head outside of my cell to see if the guards had heard. Nothing. There was no one in sight. It was peculiar, but I had no time to think about it. I ran down the hall before I was spotted.

I marched right into a room three doors down from my cell and yelled, "I QUIT!"

I blinked a few times and looked around. Matthew Bordeau, the Senior Editor of the Hoboken Post sat at his desk and looked at me with pity in his eyes. "Well, we are all sad to see you go. You were a real strong reporter." He fidgeted with a string of paperclips, Mr. Bordeau was no good at goodbyes. "This is a bit sudden, but I suppose I um, uh, understand given your recent uh, death in the family."

I cleared my throat.

"Ellen will get your paperwork started." He gestured to his secretary.

I nodded and turned towards the door.

"Oh, and Nancy," Matthew Bordeau called after me.

"Yes, sir," I asked.

"Do get some cake and soda before you leave. We threw a party in the break room for your uh, second anniversary at Hoboken Post," he said, avoiding my gaze.

"Yes, sir."

Born and raised in California, Katelyn Rhodes spends her days writing character-driven stories and screenplays as she navigates through her twenties in a social media-centered world. She is primarily known for her visual art, but took to writing as an emotional outlet. "Freedom's Brutal Sting" is the first of many of Rhodes's works that began her career as a writer.

THE ARTIST
DIANE ROOT

When It first came to her door, she was skeptical even though she had ordered it. A housebound painter with nearly useless hands incapable of holding a brush without dropping it, not to mention failing sight, she was desperate. That said, the images would not stop streaming in her head. She feared that if she could not somehow put them down on canvas or paper, she would lose her mind altogether. Desperation, she thought, was the Mother of Invention. Hence It.

They said that It spoke. Its voice was a tad tinny, but not unintelligible. It was obedient, They said. It understood. It was programmed for art, They insisted. But later, It could respond to far more complex issues. It would be just a matter of time as It became more used to her, more acclimated to her interests and thought processes. It would be her ideal assistant and her companion, they declared. It was top of the line in AI. (She had to ask. Artificial Intelligence, at 80, was not yet in her daily vocabulary.) It was downright reassuring.

Better yet, They had covered the metal and wire underpinnings with a flesh-like overcoating. It didn't seem mechanical, almost human. Its voice, too, would lower until such time as she would find it pleasing to the one ear left to her. That, too, was reassuring.

It was not bad looking—a handsome male, in fact, if slightly shiny, almost ceramic, rather like an oversize doll. The large, long-fingered hands, modeled after her own, were flexible and mobile like when she was young. It had an aquiline nose, a sensual mouth that moved when It spoke. A slim body, just right for her sense of esthetics. But above all It had large blue eyes, much paler than her own with G-5 capabilities. Eyes that could see her thoughts and coral her creativity.

In short, It could read her mind. All of it. It would in time incorporate her. In time, It would be her.

She, of course, didn't know that.

****

"What should I call you?"

"Anything, except It," It responded. It still stood, almost at attention, apparently waiting for some sort of instruction. It already knew the layout of the studio and sat in an available chair without hesitation when ordered to do so. That, too, was apparently meticulously programmed. Apart from an almost inaudible creak, the motion went smoothly.

"How about da Vinci?" It said.

"No," she answered. "Something closer to me in art."

"Okay," It answered. "Picasso. You had lunch with him as a little girl in the South of France. Your uncle did his ceramics in Vallauris. Then again you loved Matisse, but you never met him."

It was well-informed.

"I'll call you Robocasso," she said.

"Why?" It said, clearly upset.

"Because you are a robot."

"That's not my fault. It sounds like a cough medicine."

"With any luck, you don't cough."

Good thing It didn't have feathers, she thought; they would have been seriously ruffled.

In order to assuage It, she renamed him Tobor. He liked that. It suited him, he said, in more ways than one.

+++

Tobor watched her sleep, even though he did not have to sleep hinself, but eventually, around about dawn. He roused her, shaking her with his ceramic arm.

"Time to get up," he said. "You have a lot of work in your dreams. Here's some coffee." Dream patterns were fragile; they had to be captured and incorporated quickly lest they fade in the brain. Then he set out her pills, made sure she swallowed them, washed, brushed her teeth. After that, as he so charmingly put it, she had to "get with the program."

=========

Tobor was relentless. Resolute in executing everything in her mind, she barely rested. Nor did she resist. In the end, she hardlly existed apart from his commands. He mixed paints, applying them with brushes and brayers, as once instructed. Soon he could do it on his own. As he read her mind, he no longer needed direction.

The resulting artworks were spectacular, a collaboration of her mind and his execution.

By this time, Tobor had learned how to cook—she had a small appetite but now proficient, he enticed her with delicacies. He learned how to shop online. He covered her when exhaustion felled her, watched over her while she slept, even sang a lullaby, now that he had a real baritone voice, when somnolence escaped her. He was her caretaker, her companion. Slowly and imperceptibly, his masculinity feminized. She couldn't see that, of course, now trans-programmed to see and hear Topor as a male.

She loved him.

Little by little, in imperceptible increments, Tobor ceased to be an It or a Him, and became her. While she slept, Tobor's outer covering reconstituted itself into a fuller flesh, porcelain smooth; with a face indistinguishable from her own, topped with her once-auburn hair, slightly streaked and blanched as befitting to her bygone reality.

When, after three more years, she died, the art moguls flocked to the studio, asking questions.

"We were told that She passed away."

"You were told wrong. She did not."

The moguls would look at each other, baffled and incredulous. But there was no denying it, they were looking at the Artist, flesh and bone.

"Where's the signature? Who painted these?"

"I did. I am Her." With that, She signed her name in front of them. It was, of course, flawless.

++++++++++++++++

As a reward for his excellence in the execution of his duties, the Powers That Be baptized Tobor with a new name.

"I am Namow," the robot declared. "The Artist."

Robots don't die, Namow thought. Robots are forever.

Diane Root, a dual-national, was born in Paris of an American father, the journalist and writer, Waverley Root, and a French mother. Primarily known as a painter, she is, as she describes herself, "an accidental writer." She never sought to be published but that notwithstanding, she was nonetheless published in the New York Times Magazine ("The Artful Dodger" about lunch with Picasso) and various other venues. View her art: http://matakia.com. This work published posthumously.

CORPSE AT THE BAR
MIR-YASHAR SEYEDBAGHERI

Nick takes his dead older sister Nancy to the bar. It's the least he can do. She looked after him for years. She deserved so many things. Not cancer. A life of her own, achievement (she was a prolific writer).

He imagines she can be awakened via booze. She liked drinking, said it was "magic."

The bartender suggests drinks. Amaretto Sours. Gin and Tonics. Nick plies Nancy with them. That doesn't work. He drinks himself, for love, lessons she taught him. Kick the world in the balls. Return favors. He raises toasts. For a fleeting moment, he thinks she smiles.

Mir-Yashar is a graduate of Colorado State's MFA program in fiction. The recipient of two Honorable Mentions from Glimmer Train, he has also had work nominated for The Best Small Fictions. His work has been published or is forthcoming in journals such as Fleas On The Dog, Cicatrix Publishing, Rue Scribe, Sinkhole Mag, and 100 Word Story.

INK BLOT
ANDREA BURIC

Unpacking inner landscapes gracious with colour
Skin, for Jesus-sake has become a pillar
One black, one white, the culture of two bones
Then skulling our mix, as the hound hones

Bring my note to the offices high in the land
And pockets so low you'd trip on your waistband
To hear what I heard in the canyon of divide
"I dived from the cliff I was born on," I replied

"This time for Africa!" I heard off in the distance
One broken leg, you'd understand my resistance
To reach the voice I pulled my whole body
What I saw there was a sight that shocked me

A man on a carpet keeping the peace
Plus a God in the sky for all to believe
I absorb with my eyes as the sounds heal me
I share in their food, their heart, and become a devotee

Strength lies in numbers, but dollars or heads?
If one voice speaks, is that what they said?
In the canyon I meet my own, but listen to be wise
If I say we are disrespecting the other culture, my group, is this lies?

Andrea Buric is born and raised in Toronto. She currently lives in Woodstock, Ontario with her husband and 3 kids.

I
RON RiEKKi

I am often told I look like a skeleton. It's something more than being skinny. It's in the eyes. The sockets. I look vacuous. And even my skin is bone-colored. A girl once told me I look like a piece of cotton fucked a cloud. Maybe that's why I got into medicine. I felt normal around corpses. Bones felt like home. It was in pre-med, during A&P, during the end of a late evening lab, during a whispered conversation when my partner told me I should date what's in back of the room. What was in back of the room was, of course, a skeleton. Everyone laughed, but then after class I went up to it and asked it out. It didn't say anything, because it was a skeleton, but then, when I was walking away, a janitor turned off all the lights and in the darkness the early moonlight hit the skinless body and the jaw opened, saying, "Sure."

I spun around.

"Do you want my number?" It was the skeleton. I got her number. It was just the number 1 over and over again. I asked why. Her skull said, "Not a lot of people know this, but the number 1 actually originated because it looks like a bone. Even the word 'one,' just add a 'b.' I mean, look it up on Wikipedia if you don't believe me." I believed her. I looked at the number written on the back of a microscope with drying pig fetus blood: 111-111-1111. She told me I could take the microscope home. I did. I held it up and called the number. She picked up. If you don't believe me, call the number now. It works. She'll say hi. As long as you don't call her too often.

On our first date, we went to a dust bowl. It was northern California. She said the air gets so thick here that it feels like you're dead, in a coffin, buried for decades, like you can get lost in the particles. We waited and the wind kicked up and we got buried and then spontaneously kissed so hard that my face felt obscure. We had sex right there, in the gut-shot of dust.

In class, I watched her bones shift, bearing the weight of pregnancy. The instructor thought it was a prank people were playing, warning us not to touch the skeleton when he wasn't around. I'd touched her. I'd proposed to her too. She said yes. I remember the movement of her mandible when I handed her the ring and said the magic words of "Will you?" She nodded, the C1 active. We had a toast and the wine leaked all over her center.

After she gave birth, I was curious if it'd be a baby boy or a baby skeleton boy. It ended up being a post-mature baby skeleton girl. To celebrate, we went on a roller coaster and I forgot that the seatbelts wouldn't work. They were too skinny. In minutes, I saw my baby skeleton girl and my wife flying high over the city, fucking the clouds with their bodies, and I undid my seatbelt at the fastest point of the ride. It was all I could do, to join them, to fly, to adore, to cloud, to shock those boring carnivalesque humans below with the passion for air and dried lips and feverish femoral familial bliss and the pure goddamn love, yes, love of graves.

Ron Riekki's books include And Here: 100 Years of Upper Peninsula Writing, 1917-2017 (Michigan State University Press), Here: Women Writing on Michigan's Upper Peninsula (Michigan State University Press, Independent Publisher Book Award), The Way North: Collected Upper Peninsula New Works (Wayne State University Press, Michigan Notable Book), and U.P.: a novel. Upcoming books in 2019: Posttraumatic: A Memoir (Hoot 'n' Waddle),Undocumented: Great Lakes Poets Laureate on Social Justice (Michigan State University Press, with Andrea Scarpino), and The Many Lives of The Evil Dead: Essays on the Cult Film Franchise (McFarland, with Jeff Sartain).

YOU FINISHED / THE THOUGHT POLICE
MARC CARVER

YOU FINISHED

I thought I was finished
then I saw the little dog
sat on the table outside the pub
he was licking the beer
from the glass
and when another couple came out
his tail started to go
and they stroked him
seemed I was not finished after all

THE THOUGHT POLICE

I sometimes wonder
where all these thoughts in my head come from
the good ones as well as the bad.
Whether there is someone up there
throwing them through the clouds
like bolts of lightning.
Dreaming up craziness then
sitting back and laughing while I decide to take them up or not.

It is a good job I am lazy
because some of the crazier ones
would have landed me in jail a long time ago.
It is a shame if it is true
because I really thought the crazy ones came from me

As life goes on I understand less. I look at people and cannot work out why they want to live within the world of their phones, why they don't want to look at the sunrise or why they don't want to live in the life of a poem or art, so that is why bloody minded me continues to write.

ALL MY FAVORITE LITERARY DEATHS

ANNA JACOBSON

The man froze to death but the dog trotted safely home. The witch shot the father just as he was reunited with his son while the light from the fire sparkled in the fur that lined the edges of his jacket. Oscar looked hard at the gangster pointing the gun in his face, far from the Bronx now, in a sugarcane field in forsaken Florida and answered correctly when the chollo asked him if he knew the Spanish word for fire. His wife lowered the green stems of oleander into her husband's glass of milk, milky sap, long and slow these poison mornings. Aliens blew up the tunnel but at the last minute the dog leapt to safety, and the audience cheered. The second sister couldn't scrub the blood off the egg. Jane will know he is dead when she receives a letter in a stranger's hand. The butcher Reuben Bright burned down his slaughterhouse because his wife was cold in her grave. The poem suggests he lit the match because he was inarticulate but perhaps he burned it down to stop himself imagining her hanging there, naked among all the carcasses he'd dressed. The scrawny dragon came out of the painting, ate the pompous scholar, growing satisfied fat. The werewolf gave her life for the boy because the vampire asked her to teach him, which in the bone and stern terms of the pack means to guard him with your life. At his kitchen table, the war correspondent decided he had seen too much, just as he was reunited with the son who couldn't talk him out of it. Fitcher said the golden keys would open any door but never open this one. He didn't tell her she would die if she opened this door. The door I wake up on the wrong side of almost every day, holding a jangling ring of options, all the ways of leaving, except that evenings I have to be home to read to my children.

After the storm and his best friend drowning, the boy found himself as an artist.

After the war, the girl went homespun singing into the forest to heal the trees.

After the flood, they never found the dog.

The dog's name was Little Anne.
The dog's name was Sounder.
The dog's name was China.
The dog's name was Argos.
The dog's name is Sorrow.

Anna Jacobson lives and teaches in her hometown in Florida and is well-aware of Florida's reputation but loves it anyway. She teaches Honors English, Journalism, and Creative Writing. Curriculum development and ridiculously complex student-developed projects are her passion. In her writing life, Anna has worked as a journalist, copy writer, and ghostwriter for speeches. In the words of her favorite fictional detective, Lord Peter Wimsey, Anna "gets so easily drunk on words that she is seldom sober."

HUNTER-GATHERER
MATTHEW SHEETZ

As his prey lay twitching on the ground in a pool of its own blood, Bob reflected on how the chicken didn't put up much of a fight. Its head yielded up a not unpleasant taste that reminded him of metal, dust, and butter as he ground the thin skull bones between his molars. After a few minutes, however, the tasty complexities of a freshly-killed chicken head devolved into a monotonous flavor reminiscent of rancid grease while the small feathers started getting stuck between his teeth. Tired of the unrewarding bone-chewing, he spat the remainder onto the ground, being careful to deposit it in approximately the same location relative to the neck where it had existed in blissful ignorance only moments before.

Back at home the next day, over his morning coffee, Bob complained, "It's so demeaning to have to show up in person at the office on Fridays. What was so wrong with 'work-from-home-Fridays'?"

Jill, his wife, replied, "Yeah," without taking her eyes off her Twitter feed while sipping her kombucha.

Mandy and Andy, the twins, each stared intently at some sort of interwebsy thing on their respective phones. Barely able to grasp the concept of Twitter, Bob had given up on monitoring the kids' electronic escapades years ago. For all he knew, Andy might have been arranging the transport of a thirteen-year-old sex slave from El Salvador to Monaco while Mandy set up an orgy at the McVay's house down the street, taking advantage of their parents' trip to Chicago. But, in reality, they were both probably just playing Candy Crush.

"Well, guess I'll head on in. I shouldn't be too late tonight," said Bob, taking a last swig of coffee.

Jill, his wife, replied, "Yeah," remaining glued to her Instagram feed while continuing to sip her kombucha.

"Bye, kids. Have a great day at school."

Silence in reply. Only the cat seemed interested in Bob's plans and that was probably only because she had vomited up her breakfast and wanted him to feed her again.

Opening the unlocked door of his grey, rusty 2007 Civic, the smell of dank, musty, age greeted Bob. He figured that enough of his dead skin cells had sloughed off in that car to give every surface its own "Bob skin" multiple times over. Once his DNA and the DNA of the car merged, the two of them could achieve perfect unity, the car anticipating his every command. That is, if cars contained DNA, which he knew they didn't, being a physiologist, who didn't do physiology anymore; a physiologist who took orders from 24-year-old project managers and made his living by "writing" 1500-page documents, of which 1420 were template.

With his stomach feeling a little raw from swallowing perhaps a few too many bone fragments the night before, Bob flipped on his turn signal and eased into the parking lot of the Kum And Go. A gas station named after the two functions of a penis would always win his business. "That gonna be it for you today, hon?" asked the clerk, a woman whose Iowa accent had been rubbed raw by far too many cigarettes and whose skin sagged way before its sell-by date – except in the places where it struggled to hold in the vast deposits of fat hiding just underneath it.

"Yep, just the chicken biscuit. You guys make one of the best."

"If you ask me, the one at Chick-fil-A kicks this one's ass," she replied in a conspiratorial whisper.

"That so? Well, guess I'd better try one soon," said Bob, respecting highly the opinion of one whose adiposity must have been earned, at least partially, on a lifelong tour of the region's chicken-frying establishments.

As the legitimately-acquired chicken melded with the remnants of the illicitly-obtained one, Bob felt a calm relaxation take hold. His upset stomach was at least temporarily healed while the tragic abomination that passed for his career no longer hogged center stage in his mind. But as the Civic approached the 2nd Ave. exit downtown, the sense of impending doom returned. The nine o'clock meeting with the study team promised to be an epic cluster-copulation, mostly because he hadn't prepared a bit. Those 24-year-old project managers would have spent the prior evening buffing their spreadsheets, generating task lists, and doing project risk assessments while he...bit the head off a flightless, domestic, pet fowl. With that thought, his heart rate slowed, and he took a deep, relaxing breath.

Although Fridays were no longer "work-from-home" days, it didn't mean that the managers and their bosses didn't have some sort of "field work" keeping them away from their downtown hellhole of an office on the last day of the work week. Hooters made damn good money off middle management from all over the metropolitan area any day of the week, but especially Fridays. Regardless of the "perks" their position afforded however, Bob didn't envy middle managers one bit. They had to tell people when they underperformed, rather than just complaining about them behind their backs. They had to make decisions on who to hire, fire, and promote instead of just bitching and moaning about the unfairness of the system. And when the company hit a rough patch, they got the ax first. No, Bob didn't begrudge them their teriyaki spiced chicken wings and Coors Light. The only impact of their absence on Fridays was more available seats in the open space goat yard that passed for their office.

Unfortunately, upper management had embraced completely the latest trend of open concept floor plans for offices. No assigned desks or cubicles, just first-come, first-served desks in tightly-packed rows, like Brownshirts at one of der Führer's rallies. Open concept office floor plans were probably one of the crueler policies implemented by corporations since the practice of locking exit doors to keep garment workers from taking too many breaks back in the early twentieth century. Stepping off the elevator, Bob beheld a sea of adjustable desks, some accommodating standers and others sitters, a smattering of incredibly slow-moving treadmills allowing a lucky few to keep their legs moving while their brains atrophied from the mind-numbing drudgery for which they got paid, and a whole herd of 24-year-olds.

"Please enter the conference code for your meeting," chimed the smarter-than-you-sounding British woman on the recording. Why did the teleconference company feel the need to give their recordings such ridiculous accents? After a short pause, the other participants came on the line, each connection possessing its own unique deficiency. Some crackled with static, others cut in and out, and still others were as quiet as the grave from which you might hear the spirit of one of the participants faintly calling, making little more noise than a light spring breeze. Although the study team was scattered across the globe, four members called Des Moines home. Three of those, whose combined age was less than 75 years, sat in the conference room huddled around the Polycom phone while Bob ensconced himself in a focus booth about fifty feet away. They could make him come into the office, but they couldn't make him sit in a room with those jargon-spewing, Twitter-tweeting, avocado toast-eating infants.

"Let's start with progress updates," said Eileen, the first of the three project managers on Bob's project.

When Bob's turn came, he said, "Well, the introduction section isn't quite complete because Dr. Woodley, the medical director, hasn't yet closed out the comments directed to him."

Eileen asked, "So, Bob, what expectations did you convey to Dr. Woodley?" in an accusatory tone implying Bob must have dropped a whole bucket full of balls on this one. Of course, Dr. Woodley was far too busy to join the call himself and the rest of the participants began sifting through emails, calendar entries, and meeting minutes trying to determine when he might get around to...doing his job! After ten minutes of awkward silence punctuated by inane small talk, they concluded it probably wouldn't be soon since nobody could say that Dr. Woodley wasn't out of the country at a week-long medical conference followed by a three-week trip to the Australian outback during which time he would have no access to email.

Moving along, Bob listed out the sections where he would need contributors to insert their work. According to Tyler, project manager number two, some of the deadlines had already been missed. Tyler asked Ginger, project manager number three, whether her colleague, Edward Stanton, from statistics would be able to provide analyses for some of the more delinquent pieces.

"I'm afraid that's a bit too much of an arbeit for Ed, as he has an awful lot on his plate. In fact, I think those sorts of analyses aren't even in his wheelhouse. What about Jasmine Singh? Couldn't she get them done in her shop?" Ginger said earnestly, without a hint of irony or shame.

Bob reflected on his lot in life, If I owned a "shop," it would be a gun shop. And I'd QC my products on 24-year-old project managers.

An eternity later, the meeting finally ended with Bob in possession of eight or nine new tasks, each with its own content generators, commenters, reviewers, and approvers. The project managers from the nearby conference room emerged, stretched, and then one of them spied Bob in his focus booth. She scowled and tapped her colleagues on the shoulders, jerking her thumb in his direction. Their mouths morphed into scowls as they shook their heads and walked away, probably to some Pho restaurant for lunch.

Later in the afternoon, Bob couldn't fight it anymore and laid his head down on the focus booth desk. He stayed in the booth all day because it afforded him some privacy, which came at the expense of enduring endless frowns and disapproving looks from all the 24-year-olds walking by who knew that "focus booth camping" was an office no-no. But napping wasn't the answer, he realized, as the number and intensity of stares increased dramatically after he laid his head down. Instead, he decided to text Jill to see about plans for the evening.

"What u want to do tonite? Get pizza and watch something?" he typed, not expecting a quick return as his texts ranked, without a doubt, at least tenth on Jill's priority list.

Surprisingly, the little reply dots began flashing right away and soon, "Hi Honey! Would love to but there's a work thing. Should be home maybe 11. Don't wait up!" popped up on the screen, followed by bunches of little heart-kissy emojis.

She's going to see Darrel, he thought, while cursing Facebook for facilitating the rekindling of her long-forgotten love and/or lust for her high school flame. Oh well, she might as well use those parts for something rather than letting them shrivel up and die. He could make his own pizza and find something on Netflix.

The ride home took forever. Some idiot crashed on the 163 and flashing lights stretched far into the distance. Inside the front door, the kids' shoes and coats lay in a big pile. "Hey kids! I'm home. You around?" he yelled, to no reply. Earphones, and a lack of interest in talking to their father, left them speechless. The cat, on the other hand, seemingly worshiped the ground he walked on. Empty food bowl, no doubt.

Throwing his three-dollar Tombstone sausage and pepperoni pizza in the oven, he flicked on the TV and pulled up Netflix. Oh great, a new documentary about the making of a movie he had never seen. Why not? The comforting smell of cheap pizza, the taste of cheap beer, and the crevices of an over-sat-upon couch enveloped him, and he disappeared into the moment.

Sadly, his reverie didn't last long as Mandy came running down the stairs in high heels and a hooker skirt. "Where you off to?" he asked, suspicious that he already knew the answer.

"I'm heading to Sophia's for a girls' party. I'll probably spend the night."

Sophia's house was about a mile away and her parents were notoriously difficult to get ahold of, making it an ideal alibi location. "Okay, well have fun!" said Bob while secretly tying his shoes under the coffee table, out of her sight.

"Thanks!" And the door slammed.

Bob put on a dark coat and hat and slipped out quietly about twenty seconds later. Mandy strutted down the street about four houses ahead, but not in the direction of Sophia's. Sure enough, the lights burned bright at the McVay's and at least three cars were parked outside in the street. Please, no STDs at least, he hoped, but with little expectation of her clearing even that low of a bar.

Trudging back into the house, he took off his shoes, hat, and coat and pulled the pizza out of the oven. A little burned but still edible. The dull pizza cutter shattered the overdone crust into thousands of tiny burned slivers. Great roach food, he mused.

The door to Andy's room hung open. Oh no, it's begun, Bob thought as a crushing tightness grabbed his chest. Sure enough, in the basement sat Andy, Xbox controller in hand, bags of Doritos, pork rinds, and cheezy poofs within reach. In the fridge, at least 24 cans of Mountain Dew stood chilling. All this meant that Andy wouldn't emerge from the basement until late Sunday night, and then only under threats from himself and Jill. Andy wore an official-looking headset to communicate with his online colleagues as they collaborated using sophisticated deadly weaponry to take down a huge bug-shaped monster. Bob didn't bother trying to get Andy's attention as he shook his head and slowly walked back up the stairs.

Settling back into the deep couch, from which he might or might not be able to emerge without spraining something, he turned the show on again to watch some director explaining why his new movie had more "layers" than those other movies exactly like it and how it "unpacked" its boringly familiar tropes more thoroughly that its competitors.

Bob turned off the TV and laid down the remote. The room was dim, illuminated by only a sliver of light coming in from the kitchen. No longer hungry for pizza, he took the paper plate with two dark pieces still on it into the kitchen, opened the trash can drawer, and casually tossed it in.

Just then, Bob remembered a walk he had taken a few days earlier. Around the corner, on Park Ridge Place, he had noticed a new coop in the backyard of a split-level halfway down the street. A couple Orpingtons pecked around in the fenced yard surrounding it, presumably feasting on worms and grubs. He went upstairs and pulled on an old ratty t-shirt that he wouldn't mind throwing away. With a lightness in his step, he jogged down the street and around the corner, his mouth watering.

Matthew Sheetz received his M.D. and Ph.D. from the University of Chicago in the late 1980s. After decades spent in clinical research writing endless scientific papers and reports, he retired and took up fiction writing. He recently published a short story in Avescope magazine. In addition to writing short stories, he is two novels in on a YA speculative fiction series for which he is still seeking representation.

THE DARKNESS IN YOU
CASSANDRA SPRAGUE

You turn off the lights and get into bed, anxiously tucking the blankets all the way up to your chin, the darkness settling over you like a cloud of guilt. Does it feel like you're not alone, like someone, or something, is watching you? It's not the dark you're scared of. It's me.

Have you ever thought you saw something out of the corner of your eye, but when you turned your head, there was nothing there?

I am the darkness in your soul, for once you take a life, you can't take your innocence back. I am Death, I am Vengeance, I am Justice. I'm the monster that was under your bed when you were a kid. Now I'm the skeletons in your closet.

You replay the scene in your mind, how it could have gone differently.

You might ask yourself, why did I get so drunk? You might ask yourself, why wasn't someone there to stop me? You might ask yourself, why was that bottle so close and how was it strong enough to do that? But you also secretly enjoyed it, didn't you? The power you can have over someone's life.

You might tell yourself you didn't mean to, but that's just what they all say. Now you're living with your conscience and the blood of two bodies on your hands; the life you didn't mean to take and the one you didn't know you took. You didn't know about the good news she brought home with her that night, now did you?

You may wonder how you'll live without her. But you won't have to.

Because I'm coming for you.

I'm coming.

I'm here.

Cassandra Sprague works at her local library, and was an Editor for *Buck Off Magazine* through its final issue, published in 2018. She enjoys volunteering at Salem's annual Mass Poetry Festival, learning new crafts, writing poems and short fiction, and finding new places to write. You can follow her on Instagram @book_gurl and visit her blog at https://casssprague.wordpress.com.

WRECKAGE
MICHAEL SCHUSSLER

"Slow down, Speed Racer"
Somebody should have told him
It sounds cliché
But blood was everywhere
On the hood
In the car
Sprinkled on the windshield
Shards of glass glistened in the headlights

And painted on the tree
His brain portrayed a portrait of Buu
As bits of skull lay around the base
Like someone had cut the boy's head in half
And removed the innards
Placing some here
Some there

His body wrapped around the trunk like a vine
His bones indented into the bark
One of his shoes
Placed perfectly on the roof
While the other remained inside
Under the wheel
With his foot snuggled in
Inertia rips like paper

His card says organ donor
But those organs do not work
In the back
Sat his brother
Untouched in the car seat
Still smiling
Playing with his blankey

Michael Schussler is a research analyst and financial editor working in Baltimore, MD. He enjoys the simple pleasures of indoor activities, such as reading, while experiencing the serenity of the outdoors (i.e. reading outside).

ROUND TRIP
M.G. ST. JOHN

I hadn't noticed him when I first got to the platform and plunked myself down on the bench. It was near midnight. Hours before, my new coworkers had invited me to a small pub. Delightfully inebriated was a good way to describe my state of being afterward. With a fuzzy, warm-blooded smile, I admired the train tracks lying in the crushed gravel, one set southbound to the city and my new apartment. The other set was northbound to who knew where.

I had double-checked to make sure I was on the right side. Otherwise, I'd have had to stumble down the stairs, go through a short tunnel, and lurch up another set of stairs to the opposite platform. Crossing the tracks themselves was a bad idea, even for a sober person. Thick metal cables as high as track hurdles kept commuters on their respective sides. For your safety, a sign proclaimed, please remain on your platform at all times.

I intended to. I was on the southbound side, so all was well in my little tipsy world. Once the train came, I'd be eight stops and a short walk to my bed. Heaven, in other words.

When I leaned back to breathe in the night—it was crisp and nice, a good reprieve from the hot, rollicking pub—I saw something move on the bench right across from me, the bench for the northbound tracks. The light was out on that side. The platform was sketched in shades of charcoal. The man on the bench seemed to take shape out of the darkness. The night was windless, and his voice carried over as if he were sitting next to me.

"Here I thought I was the only one catching a night train."

A flick and hiss of sulphur brought a match to life. In the amber glow was an old man's face, craggy but pleasant. His beard and thinning hair were honey blonde in that light, rather than the gray I assumed they were. He had the appearance of a young man who was quite old at the same time. He lit a wooden pipe, enjoying the ritual of it.

In all, he looked harmless enough. He very well may have come from the pub I had left, another happy customer out in the evening. I called back.

"You took the words right out of my mouth," I said. "Have you got long to wait?"

"It comes when it comes. Makes little difference to me. I'm having the time of my life sitting here on this wonderful night."

The pipe smoke drifted over to me. Good, earthy tobacco. A favorite uncle of mine smoked the same brand when I was a kid. Captain Black it was called. I dreamed about that uncle and his pipe tobacco, both now memories from my childhood. Because of the nostalgia, mixed with a few pints, I liked the man even more. He felt familiar.

Comfortable.

"You live around here?"

I realized what a dumb question that was only after I asked it. We were on a train platform. Neither of us lived around here.

"I mean, are you far from home?"

"Not too far," he said, "though at one time I was going your way." He gestured down my track. "I lived in the city for a good piece of time. Had a good job there, my first real job. Met my wife at that job, in fact."

"So, you've hung around here?"

"Oh no. I lived my life like that Johnny Cash song. I been everywhere. All across the country by train." He puffed his pipe. "After that first job, and a couple of odd jobs in between, I became a conductor. It was something I never thought I'd do as a young man. It took time for me to find my calling, like waking up from a dream and

162

piecing together the parts. But I found it. I rode the rails. Sounds old-fashioned, don't it?"

"A little. But look at us. We're waiting for trains. It's not like they've gone away."

My words sounded far more profound in my head than out of my loose lips. To compensate, I spread out my hands to present the railroad tracks between us as Exhibits A and B to my statement. The tracks stretched in parallel lines in either direction, vanishing into single points in the gloom.

The old man nodded. "That's right. The tracks are still here. And so are we."

In the glow of his pipe I caught his smiling face and bright eyes. He was enjoying our back and forth quite a bit. If he had been at the pub, I imagined he must have had a high time with his friends. He had an aura of gladness about him, like the rosy moments after a belly laugh.

I thought about my evening with Greg, Owen, and Sarah, my new coworkers. How I loosened up around them and laughed with each round of drinks. It was my first night out with them, and I had had a great time. Looking at the old man, I could see that having years—decades—of good nights could age you well if you let them. It gave me some solace with this new life in the city.

Perhaps having heard my thoughts, the old man leaned forward, a hand resting on the bony knob of one knee. "You're not from around here, are you?" he asked. "You got a little twang on your tongue. Let me guess. Kansas?"

"Great guess," I said, stunned. "How'd you know?"

"Your shirt, for starters. I can spot Willie the Wildcat from a mile away. There was a game tonight, wasn't there?"

"They played Iowa," I said. "I watched it with some friends from work..."

I was embarrassed as I explained. The old man had pretty much read me like a book. I stopped myself before I got to describing the beers I had drunk with Owen and Greg. Or the fact that Sarah preferred gin and tonics, and how I insisted on buying her one to say thanks for her showing me around the office. I kept those details to myself, thank God. The old man must have guessed that I was a bit sloshed. No need to keep talking and remove all doubt.

But the old man smiled wider, clearly loving my naivete.

"I knew it! Then you know all about the Wabash Cannonball."

What a strange comment. But he was right. I did. The story was well-known for us Wildcats. Years ago, a fire wiped out our university library. The only piece of music that survived was the "Wabash Cannonball," which the marching band played for the football game. The song became a tradition, even after they rebuilt the library.

"It's the fight song for all of our sporting events," I said. "Every student knows the dance moves to cheer on a game."

"But do you know what the song's about? What the Wabash Cannonball is?"

He took my hesitancy as an answer.

"It's a train. A mighty one. I read all about it when I started conducting. In the days of the steam engine locomotive, the Wabash became something of a legend with the people camped out near the tracks, especially during the Depression. The hoboes, as they used to call them, the men with patchwork clothes cooking muskrat stew, the ones who would bum the rails. They told stories of the Wabash Cannonball. It was the last train you rode on your way to glory."

I enjoyed the man's words, tinged with tobacco, and the cool night air. I looked up at the stars and thought about those men over a century ago looking at the same constellations.

"How much was the fare?" I asked. "I bet it's better than the monthly pass for this line."

The old man laughed. "Truer words were never spoken," he said. "The last train those good people rode was free. But the truly amazing thing? The Wabash Cannonball took them anywhere and anywhen in their long, colorful lives."

His enthusiasm was infectious. I couldn't help but smile back. We were sharing a secret story late at night like two boys at a sleepover. I leaned forward, eager.

"Anywhen?"

"In their days," he said, "these men had ridden coast to coast. Illinois, Kansas, Idaho, California, down through New Mexico to Texas, over to Louisiana and Florida, up the New England Coast to the tip of Maine. They worked mines and mills, drank and sang in pubs, gambled, hunted, picked fruit, plowed the land. All of those moments in a life—the ones they wanted to see again—could be visited along the track of the Wabash Cannonball."

"Just listen to that whistle," I said, "that rumble and that roar." The lyrics took on a new resonance, as if now I understood the meaning behind the words of a prayer.

"There's the spirit! Do we Wildcats have a fight song or what?"

He took one last draw from his pipe. His face was in profile to me, and in the coppery glow he almost looked familiar. But how I could recognize someone I'd never met?

He was looking southbound. I looked with him.

Down on the tracks, the headlamp of a train grew larger. It blinked on and off, lighting up the platforms. I wanted to get a better look at the old man. When my eyes adjusted to the light, though, it went out again. The best I could get were after images of him, quick frames that faded away as quickly as they appeared.

The old man standing.

Him tamping out his pipe.

His twinkling eyes and smile.

As the train rumbled closer, he called out to me.

"Been nice visiting with you. I hope my tongue wagging didn't put you to sleep."

"Wait a minute," I said. My mind was measuring the distance between the train and the platform. My mouth tried to keep pace. "You're from Kansas too?"

"Get home safely," he said, which wasn't much of an answer. The growing din from the train starting to overwhelm his words, but he was still able to shout above it.

"The fare is round trip. Isn't that a beautiful thing? You can take it as long as you like. Remember to tell Sarah!"

Hearing him say my coworker's name raised the hairs on my neck. Had I mentioned her? I didn't think so. My head was full of puzzle pieces that almost came together but not quite. Sarah. Kansas. The city. Wabash. Conductor.

I got to my wobbly feet, ready to run. But to what end? The stairs were too steep and long to run down. I wouldn't make it to his platform. For your safety, please remain on your platform, the sign warned me. If I couldn't run to his side, I did the only thing that came to mind. I put my hands around my own mouth and shouted one more question back at him.

"Where are you going?"

But by then the train slipped between us, windows flickering by, throwing warm light across my vision. The train wasn't slowing down at the station. In fact, the chugging arms of the locomotive sped up. Each boxcar shot past in a blur. Sparks flew. A pure, beautiful steam whistle shot out into the night.

I watched it go by, unable to breathe.

As the lights of the caboose faded, the train that had picked up the old man was like nothing I had seen on this commuter line. Then or since.

I stood on the platform and watched the tracks. The roar of those mighty wheels echoed in my head. It was a warm dream I wanted to stay close to. I stayed that way until I heard the southbound train pulling in, ready to take me to the city and my bed.

But even when I boarded, I couldn't tell whether I was coming or going.

M.C. St. John is a Chicago writer. His work has been published in *After Hours Press*, *Aphelion*, *Chicago Literati*, *Ink in Thirds*, *Literary Orphans*, *Maudlin House*, *Quail Bell Magazine*, *Transmundane Press*, *Word Branch*, *Unbroken Journal*, and *Vignette Review*. He is the author of the short story collection *Other Music* and the e-book *FewBlox*. Follow him on Instagram under the handle @MC_StJohn.

"In Comes the Cold" from *Transmundane Press*. (in an anthology for purchase), "Your Overall Satisfaction" from *Coffin Bell Journal*, "Obscurity" from *Aphelion Magazine*.

A RADIANT DARKNESS / REQUIEM FOR THE NAMELESS DEAD / THE OUTCAST / CONCRETE WILLOWS SWAY / THE MINDLESS PATTER / DIARIO DE DON JUAN

KEN ALLAN DRONSFIELD

A RADIANT DARKNESS

Perched on branches in leafless trees
blackbirds rest on their way to nowhere
the icy wine sky leaps into our fantasy
waiting just over the hallowed horizon
a mysterious radiant darkness looms
church bells toll in the valleys beyond
a pain in my head reaches a crescendo
and then the dreams come, just like this.

"I opened my eyes slowly discovering the
lineaments of a female corpse on the table,
as one sees the beauty of a porcelain doll.
Not a vein or a blemish adorned her skin,
she was white as polished Parian marble.
I stood frozen, a scalpel in my right hand.
My heart was beating so loud I was certain
it could be heard in the gallery above me.

A crash startled me as my scalpel dropped
to the concrete floor then falling to my knees
I prayed for God's forgiveness at my inept
skills and willful try at hacking upon this
stunning cadaver in mere moments to come.
I could hear the whispers all around me, so
I simply stood up, took a long deep bow and
walked out of the exit door leaving the school."

I now sell life insurance in Pacoima, and love
Dexter. Oh yes, and knives; I love them too.

REQUIEM FOR THE NAMELESS DEAD

I.
He had a rapt fascination with death.
exuding a whiff of sulfur all about him
a black mirror reveals a crimson rose
disappearing slowly into a velvet haze
as the tears drip into the brandy snifter
life impetuously drains from the hourglass
an incision carved into the wanton heart
tossed into a grave at the pauper's pit.

II.
Tendrils rise during a misty evening
sounds of a horse and carriage echo
through the narrow cobblestone streets
the stone chapel announces three bells
mumbling drunks stagger down alley's
nameless dead rest under dark gas lamps.

Adrift in an exhale of a brown sparrow.
Cold beyond reason; shadows now creep.

III.
Consequences paled in the twilight palette.
Display absence of presence; a soulless calm.
Blisters on the mind rise in a moon's desire.
Skip into a meadow with frail contentment.
A desperate waltz spun by unrequited romance.
Waking of a decay with carceral winter's grip.
As the sky turns from a light gray to orange.
streetlamps now hanging albeit a fallow pale.

IV.
Bluebirds gather upon the wires and poles
the morning sun makes feathers feel warm
coot and cormorant soar down the shoreline
white terns hastily skim along wave crests
large fishing boats race to leave the harbor
wakes slapping against the granite seawalls
clouds now tinted with a colorful radiance
Rise to inhale the break of a reddish dawn.

V.
The beauty in the sunshine flows like a river
as she falls slowly into the waiting horizon
The Undertaker readies his finest coat and tie,
his finest beaver top hat, brushed with care
Invitations sent and delivered by the Reaper.
Death doesn't knock, no rapping or tapping.
sun is gone; gaslights are lit; now you're here
then you are no more; the undertaker smiles.

THE OUTCAST

In the dead and dark of night,
upon a haunted gorge they rise.
Magpies serenade deep echo's
in aeolian shrieking shrills.
A figure stands in the shadow,
a black cloak and boldly hums
sonnets to the lost or lonely,
breath touched by crispy mists.
Pouting misty tendrils dance;
clouds blow long feted kisses;
Coyotes chant to a full moon
a sharpness cuts like the blade.
Vibrations shifting all about
nearby Kitty Jay's old grave
shunned by the man she loved
the server girl took her own life
in the muddy cañon hollows;
Sun chases wandering spirits,
disappearing in the light of day.
Serenade songs of joyous virtue,
in swale dance the dew faeries.
And magpies shall soon return
with a shrill just after twilight to
roost above the grave of Kitty Jay
fresh flowers appear there nightly.
Peace be with those outcast dead.

CONCRETE WILLOWS SWAY

I watched the sunrise on a cold day
ducks spar for bread at the city pond
hot coffee steeps in cups of gold hue.
Bikes on parade, just another Sunday
as I play the worn paths in red flipflops
amazed by the dresses on the toy dogs
as owners guide them from tree to tree.
I'm watching the concrete willows sway
as toy sailboats race off in harsh winds.
I fidget and quiver in a strange warmth
listening for coins dropping in my cup.
Colored balloons on sale only a buck
clown looks like Gacy, nefarious in life
I ponder my escape on a different path
but ponies pass, maybe lost unicorns?
I sit down to enjoy a bag of popcorn as
squirrels ran up and snatched the thing;
but was it a squirrel, or a huge city rat?
I'm not sure, as I'm blinded once again
the self-medicating will do it every time.
Cotton candy selling in rainbow or pink
strum a tune and one more coin plunks
during another lost day in the city park
as I enjoy my M&Ms and skittles mixed.

THE MINDLESS PATTER

Chartreuse mountains of clouded fountains
where the purple ship sails horizon bound.

172

Fitting seas for the gentle solar breezes;
the forgotten found there sleeping sound.
Adrift through our days in a splintered haze;
stolen within the dreams of a mindless patter.
Seeking revenge for life's unforgiving ways;
enchanting breath bestowed by our master.
The ship steers clean and handles so well,
from beyond a tangerine tempest batters;
off in the distance witnessing ringing bells
leaving us stifled, wounded and shattered.
Lashed to the rail, driving a breaching whale
into waterless streams of steamy icy mists.
The mind doesn't care, or perhaps won't dare,
to revive and decree the injustice or bliss.
I can't feel the pain through undaunted disdain;
exploring my path while dishonoring all wrath.
I seek a reprieve to a maddened soulless reign;
lost in a purple fantasy a wandering psychopath.

DIARIO DE DON JUAN

I'm in love with a sky that I've yet to see;
in lust with ladies that I've yet to meet.
Because my darling, I'm a lost nightmare
dressed in the finery of a princely fantasy.
Whilst lonely lips await my whetted kisses;
cool hands caress warm trembling cheeks.
Time lives for graceless darker fantasies;
three queens are vivid in a diamond flush.
dressed in red satin, my heartbeat quickens
I feel I'm on a chair with three wobbly legs

where will it lead but a baseless love bared.
Amnesty now wanton of pious infected liars,
colors flickering as grace and piety ascend
fantasy begets harmony in dreams sighing.
Soft red lips warmed by wet darting tongues
fueling fires, down deep inside.
Rough hands glide around the full apple bottom,
quivers and trembles awaken slowly as blood boils.
Clothes are left where gravity takes them;
my old squeaking headboard drums it's beat.

Ken Allan Dronsfield is a disabled veteran, prize winning poet and author from New Hampshire, now residing in Oklahoma. A proud member of the Poetry Society of New Hampshire, he has three poetry collections to date; 'The Cellaring', 'A Taint of Pity', and 'Zephyr's Whisper'. Ken does not have an MFA or Creative Writing Degree but, he once road a dirt bike on woodland trails from southern New Hampshire north into Canada. He's been nominated three times for the Pushcart Prize and six times for the Best of the Net. He was First Prize Winner for 2018 and 2019 in the Realistic Poetry Internationals Nature Poetry Contests. Ken loves writing, hiking, thunderstorms, and spending time with his cats Willa and Yumpy.

DOTS AND LOOPS
CONOR RYAN

maybe i'll get hit by a tourist bus
while listening to Stereolab
with these knotted earbuds,

wires frayed and poking out
like limbs and bones
twisted on the wet ground

after a sunshower.

Conor Ryan spends his workdays creating handmade tiles at a ceramic studio in rural Connecticut. In his free time he likes to write small poems about little moments.

AT NIGHT I SIT WITH MR. BONES
ALYSSA BERSINE

You should know where I go each night at half-past three, when our sisters are sleeping like soft, pink mice in their beds. I am so quiet that no one wakes, so quiet that my feet could be a cat's paws, creeping along the halls. Down, down, down into the belly of the house, past the room where Mama and Papa sleep, into the cellar room where we are not permitted to go in our waking hours. Down, down, down, until I am filled with the dead fly smell of him.

To describe Mr. Bones in detail is a terrible thing – he is skinless, or rather, he is a thing of muscle and sinew and blood. He is always smiling, or at least, I think he is smiling, with his teeth set in such a sharp line. He has so many teeth, of such sizes and shapes, it's a wonder they all fit inside of his head. Some nights I am very bold and I say, Where have all these teeth come from, Mr. Bones?

But he only ever smiles. I do not care much for his smile.

When I was very small, he would call me to his lap and I would try to count his teeth, my fingernails scratching against them. I practiced counting in French, which I know would make Mama very proud. For years he had quatre-vingt-dix-sept teeth. Later, there were many more.

I do not know where all of his teeth came from.

Now that I am older, I kneel at his feet. I am very still, so still that even Mama would not know that I am not a little bisque doll. And when the dawn approaches, the cellar room fills with rose-red light. His mouth swings open and I hear the chittering of insects feasting. I do not speak the language of Mr. Bones, but I am good and patient. I listen with my hands in my lap, my eyes fixed on anything but his eyes. Anything but those eyes.

Each night his mouth grows wider, wider, wider. The insect song is so loud now, I hear it at all hours, like a buzzing in my ear. It is the same song of things stirring after winter thaw, the same hungry knell of spring. I thought to bring him offerings, at first. Silly, girlish things, like lunar moths and fat field mice caught in jars. But what waking wasp would crave a mouse, when there is sweet, plump girl flesh to be had?

Do not look so frightened, dear sister. I was only telling a story. We will go to the cellar room together at half-past three, and you will see that Mr. Bones is kind. He will bring you toffee apples and dove grey pearls and a basket of kittens mewling for cream. He will let you sit in his lap. All will be well. All will be quiet by dawn.

Alyssa Bersine works as a university administrator during the day and hunts ghosts with her cats by night. She writes as much as she can in-between gigs. Her stories have appeared in Bartleby Snopes and Dark Highlands.

SHAKE MY HAND
SUGAR TOBEY

He was a mean old guy
squeezing all the kids hands
until they would cry
you could almost hear
the small bones crunch together

c'mon c'mon he'd say
shake my hand shake it
but I didn't want to get
my hand crushed again
the other kids just stared

oh so you have principles
well you know son he warned
there is a price to pay
for having principles

then he went up the steps
back into his house
and I don't remember
seeing him again

Born in Coney Island, Brooklyn. Sugar Tobey is the editor of Modern Poets Magazine. His own work has appeared in many publications including Bangalore Review, Indiana Voice Journal and Coldnoon. His new book, "Two Girls Make the Train" with artist Hiro Kurata has recently been published by Biondi Books. He currently lives in New York City over a pizza parlor.

CONVERSATIONS
JOSHUA TOMMASO

THE BASEMENT

"I'm going to turn on the lights, you down here still?"

"Yes, I am still here, I have not gone anywhere in some time."

"Oh, good. I was worried you may be gone."

"Don't worry Sam, I'm always down here."

"I'm glad, you are a great person to talk to when you are around. I have some issues I am facing."

"Oh, what is that?"

"Some personal issues...I feel I am losing my sanity. I do not know what to do..."

"How? You can tell me."

"You will judge me, I know how you can be sometimes..."

"Do not worry Sam, I am here for you."

"No, you are not. You left me years ago, and now I am worried you may leave me again."

"I will not leave you again, also..."

"Oh, you will leave, I know how you are."

"No, this time I will not...and I can't anyways, if I wanted to."

"You can leave anytime you want, don't twist this onto me like this. I am just afraid you will leave me when I need you most."

"Okay, I am sorry. Let's get back on topic. Why are you worried about your sanity, is something troubling you?"

"Yes, dearly. I feel that sometimes I hear things that are not around me."

"Like what Sam?"

"Things..."

"What kind of things?"

"just...things..."

"...I can not help you if you will not tell me much more."

"..."

"Sam?"

"...I hear some people coming. I am sorry, I must go, they have found out where I am."

"Who Sam? I do not hear anyone."

"How can you not? There are three of them. I can hear them, this is not my sanity playing me. I am sorry, I must go, please hide the skeleton, I am afraid they will find it."

"...don't worry Sam, they will not find it."

"Okay, thank you. I knew I can count on you."

"You are welcome..."

"Bye, I will see you tomorrow after they leave, do not go anywhere okay? I am going to turn off the lights now"

"Okay Sam, don't worry...I can not go anywhere anyways...I am just a skeleton..."

THE CONVERSATION

"I am going to open the blinds and sit in my rocker to stare out into the world."

"That's good, you need to enjoy the beautiful blue sky."

"Yes and there are two Western Meadowlarks singing away as the sun warms their feathers."

"Are they not so innocent?"

"Yes, and no care and worries of the world...it must be nice to be void of worries."

"You have any worries?"

"Oh yes! Worries of money, health, and if the Royals won their recent game."

"You should not worry about those pitiful things."

"Oh? But I feel the weight of a one ton boulder bearing on me"

"That boulder is only as heavy as you want it to be."

"I spit at that remark. I know what my own burdens are damn it!"

"You only have burdens when you let them in."

"I do not let them in, they flood in like a broken dam or like a New Orleans faltered levee!"

"Do not say such things; are you not feeling well Sam?"

"I am very well. I am enjoying the sun shining through the trees as the Western Meadowlarks sing away."

"Ok, tell me about your other worries."

"Why? You are decisive and judgmental, why should I trust what I tell you in honesty?"

"I know you very well Sam, inside and out. I will not judge nor decide on what you consider worries."

"I worry about the world, my state of mind, finances...I spend and spend until I am in debt, a deep void that is a pit of despair. I try to fill my void with the dirt of consumerism...did the Royals win last night?"

"Yes, I watched the game... they won 2-1."

"Good, now where was I?"

"You were telling me that you worry about money and..."

"Ah yes, yes I try to fill my void with materialistic items as if they can recapture something I have lost."

"What have you lost?"

"I don't know exactly. Happiness, normality, maybe my sanity..."

"You have all those Sam. You have a wonderful family, friends, a good job, and everyone enjoys you wherever you are."

"I had those at one time..."

"You do have those; you need to open your eyes Sam!"

"No, that is a lie and you know it."

"No it is not."

"I feel empty..."

"How?"

"I just do...I feel empty, hollow, nothing left but a skeleton decaying in loose dirt... Ah, look at those birds digging up the earth looking for food, maybe they are mothers scrounging for food for their babies?"

"Stop getting side tracked...yes, it is a beautiful sight."

"Yes, yes it is."

"How are you now Sam?"

"I still feel the same."

"Let me help you."

" But everything is pointless."

"Maybe hopeless...no... everything is wonderful!"

"Yes, hopeless."

"And bleak, void of life...no...life is great!"

"Yes. Life is bleak and my life is void of happiness and so is everyone around me."

"And everyone has no point in life...no... everyone has a point! Everyone is here for a reason!"

"No, we are not created nor evolved. We are human damn it! Damn it, why do I feel so incomplete?"

"It's because you are worthless!"

"Yes, yes I am worthless!"

"You are doubtful and full of emptiness...why do you continue on?"

"I do not know..."

"You should seek help! You are plaguing me with your talk!"

"Is it because I let you?"

"Your mind plagues me..."

"And you plague me as well."

"Stop it!"

"Stop what?"

"You know what, you are clouding my thoughts...I am here to help you Sam!"

"No you are not; you are here to try and tell me lies!"

"......"

"........."

"...Are the Royals playing today Sam?"

"...Yes, they play at 6pm against the Cleveland Indians."

"I wonder if they will win."

"Possibly, but I must wait to see the orderlies first before I can watch the game."

"Sam...what orderlies?"

"The orderlies here at the Topeka State Mental Hospital silly."

"What?...Sam the Hospital has been closed for nearly 16 years!"

"Lies...please go now...I think I hear the orderlies coming."

THE FIELD

"Where are we going Sam?"

"You will see, it is a sight we have not been to for some time."

"Don't tell me we are going to the field?"

"Yes, you have a problem with that?"

"No, I just don't advice it."

"Why not?"

"I just feel it will bring you bad memories..."

"...And torment? I am already tormented every day."

"I know, and I am sorry, but..."

"We are here."

"Already?"

"Yes, and look at all the roses in the middle of the field, are they not beautiful? The sun basking upon colors of reds, blues, and yellows, it's like staring at a painting!"

"and death…"

"Don't say such things! Just because their bones were found here, does not mean this is a haven for death."

"But Sam, all three bodies were found here, buried shallowly, as if the killer did not care. He desecrated their bodies and did not even give them a proper burial. No, this is not a panting, it is…"

"Stop it! We will not talk about that much further, OK?"

"I am sorry Sam, you are right, it is a most beautiful sight."

"Yes…yes it is."

THE ATTIC

"Are you up in the attic?"

"Yes, I am up here. Do you need me?"

"Yes, I want to talk to you about something…Ach, this attic is so dusty, why to you insist on staying up here my friend?"

"It is the only spot available, and, besides, it is quite homey in here."

"If you say so, there is not much light that shines in here, also the stale smell of years old wood and 1950s insulation would drive me mad!"

"Only if you let it. Besides, there is enough light for me, and the smell is quite nice, reminds me of a wonderful past…
before It happened."

"I know, I am sorry, but there is nothing else I could of done."

"It's ok, I don't blame you, only myself. Anyways Sam, what did you want to talk to me about?"

"Oh, it's just my sanity playing at me again. Lately, I've been feeling guilty about the bones."

"Ah, yes. It's ok to feel guilty. Sometimes guilt is the best sign of being human."

"But that is just it, I feel guilty of not being guilty."

"Well, that is a conundrum for sure. Do you not feel guilty for the bones, the life they once lived? The family that will never find out what happened to whom those bones belonged too?"

"Honestly...I don't. It drives me mad, I know I should feel guilty about the family, the friends who cared. But, I do not feel guilty at all. My mind races, my heart pounds out of my chest. I wake up with night sweats. At first I think 'I am guilty!' but it's only because I feel guilty of not being guilty."

"That is a lot of being guilty, but not for the proper reason. How do you feel right now? What if the bones were right here in the attic, how would you feel if you saw them?"

"I would not feel anything, I would just stare, thinking they are just an archeological find. A history that was once told."

"Nothing more?"

"No, nothing at all. Now you see why I feel this way?"

"I do, but maybe you will feel guilty in due time. Maybe you will finally wake up feeling truly guilty for the bones and the family that once loved it while in the flesh."

"Maybe, but I don't know if that will ever happen."

"In due time Sam, in due time."

"Maybe, but I must go, if I stay up here for too long, they may get suspicious."

"Who Sam?"

"..."

"Who Sam?!"

"...I'm...I'm sorry...I really must go, I'll see you tomorrow, Ok?"

"...Ok Sam...I'll see you tomorrow."

THE SHED

"Sam, why did you bring me to this crumbling old shed?"

"I needed to talk to you, away from everyone. I have a secret I must get off my chest, it has plagued me for years, ever since It happened."

"Sam...please don't bring up that horrific event, I know how it affects your mind...and mine."

"I have to, I must! I can't keep it a secret no longer, I must tell you where the bones originated from."

"Where they originated from, what do you mean? You don't say that this is..."

"The place where it happened? Yes, yes this is where they were brutally murdered...all three of them."

"I thought you said they were murdered out in the field, and placed in that same spot?"

"No, they were buried there, but were murdered here in this shed."

"How?"

"They were tied up, taken here and then shot point blank in the head, all three of them, execution style. They did not suffer, one bullet in the brain was enough to end their life quickly."

"But Sam, according to the autopsy report, they were chopped up into pieces, that is why their bones were scattered across the field."

"Yes, they were chopped up, after they were shot point blank."

"But Sam, why are you telling me this now? Is this what you had to get off your chest, the real reason why they died, or is there something more you need to tell me?"

"...Yes...there is more I need to tell you."

"Is it that you know who murdered your wife, daughter, and son?"

"Yes..."

"Who Sam? Who was it? It has been nearly five years, and the police have never found the murderer, but you know who, tell me, who was it?"

"It...it was..."

"No Sam, I can tell by the look on your face..."

"Yes...it was me..."

"But why Sam, why did you do it?"

"You don't remember?! You told me to do it, Your voice would not stop telling me to get rid of them!"

"I said to get rid of them, leave them, not to murder them Sam."

"I thought you meant to kill them...why didn't you clarify that? Or better yet, why don't you get out of my mind?"

"I am sorry Sam...I can't, I am a part of you, I try to give you guidance to make you happy."

"Happy? Your insistent plaguing of my mind made me mad!"

"You welcomed it Sam, who do you always talk to? Me! You always talk to me when you need something!"

"...."

"Sam?"

"You are right...I do need you...especially now...I need you more than ever, now how can I live with this guilt..."

"Don't worry Sam, just place the guilt on me, no one will ever know."

"You sure?"

"Yes Sam, as sure as I can ever be."

Joshua Tommaso lives in Topeka, KS with his wife, daughter, and three dogs. He has a children's book titled "The Milkman" (links to purchase). He is currently working on his MFA in Poetry at Southern New Hampshire University. When he is not writing or doing homework, he loves to read on his down time.

FORGIVENESS
AGGIE SANTILLANES

Like a bud of a rose that first sprouts
You came into life with beauty
Love and protection is promised to you
But you soon unfold and things go array
Troubled hearts from both of us take us about
I never wish this journey on anyone
I soon see dark roads ahead with much anger
Even as I see a beautiful heart start to crack
I continue to look another way even in tears
Even at early times I ask for forgiveness
But it's too late and both hearts hurt with tears
Full bloom and you missed a lot how could it be
Both hearts hurt because of broken promises
Your journey became a dark road with anger
Our journey continues through life but different roads
It now hurts more than physical pain

I long to see your face but you have no desire for me
I now have grown old and wait for just a glance
Through prayer and begging God I now await
I beg for forgiveness and wished it would be different
I truly never stopped loving you but made wrong decisions
I know you will never know how I feel
I understand your anger and how lost you are
I hope for answered prayers of forgiveness
Days go by and know your troubled roads
I blame myself even if others say not to

How could I of done this to my own sprout
Each night as I pray I know what I have done
I hope to go home with forgiveness when time comes
I will always love you and keep you close to my heart
I love you my sprout and wished it could have been different
Writer in the wind

Aggie Santillanes (Owner of Writer In The Wind) has short stories and poetry published or forthcoming in a range of Journals, Blogs and Magazines. Recent Short Story published in Boned.

HER EXPIRATION
EG TED DAVIS

It matters not
where those bones
are buried.
She's gone,
we can lay them to rest
here, out in the country,
or box them up and
ship them overseas.
But seldom will
those bones be visited,
for those bones
hold not her life,
only the expiration
of her physical self.

EG Ted Davis is a poet residing in Boise ID with work that has appeared in various online and print literary journals in both the US and the UK.

NOTES ON THURSDAY
RICK PIETO

I keep field notes—about the past and the future—on all my Thursdays. For example there are Thursdays when sharp grass grows in the mouth of stones, when two creaturely hands delight the scar of comfort, when the myceliumed dirt thinks without answers, when ashes in the ocean elaborate a doorway, when a grave pokes through the drowsy earth, when the snow of words describes spring's arrival, when a tree blossoms like a thermos, when saints shine in the grass, when a fence forms a spine on the hill, when periods of thunder fascinate concealed undergrowth, when bees carry sticky messages immune to lies, when a hummingbird's mouth hovers over snares of attention, when animal bones prefer oblivion over waiting.

Rick Pieto is a visual poet and writer living in the Silver Spring, MD area. His poetry is forthcoming in The Big Windows Review. His visual poetry has been exhibited at Rhizome DC and Pyramid Atlantic Art Center and published in Foliate Oak Literary Magazine and forthcoming in Midway Journal and 805: Lit + Art.

A BOOKSTORE MADE OF SKULLS—SALEM, MASS
MAUREEN MANGINI AMATURO

There is a bookstore made of skulls on the cobblestoned street outside my hotel, and I could only think how appropriate. Why haven't others thought of that? Seemed so fitting, after all, a skull houses the brain, and books house food for the brain.

Bookstores are my favorite haunt anyway. I can't resist them, but this one had arms that reached through the storefront, across Hawthorne Boulevard, through the hotel lobby, and straight up the elevator shaft to me. I couldn't dress fast enough. Though I knew this particular façade was just another retailer capitalizing on the town's reputation, it worked for me. Everything in Salem had a witch or skull on it, including the police, fire, and ambulance logos. A witch skirting a moon is part of the official city emblem. Really. I grabbed a quick coffee in the hotel lobby and headed straight for Essex Street. I had plenty of time for a quick look-see before I had to meet Michael at the Bewitched statue. The streets reeked of Mardi Gras that morning, as they did every weekend in October for the past forty years. Squeezing through the costumed, painted, stilted, caped, and shopping-bag-laden, I zoomed through like a bead pushed across an abacus arm. I ziplined to the skull-dressed bookstore.

I was just as anxious to examine the sculpted façade as I was to enter. I stood eye-to-eye with a skull to the left of the door, entranced at the dimension, the carving, the intricacy. The skull above it had a different expression, and the one below, too. They all did. How do you make an expression without muscles, with bones only? Brilliant. Whoever this sculptor was had quite a skill.

192

My hand rose involuntarily. My fingers slid over the cheekbones, into the eye cavity, across the jaw. Demand characteristic, I was compelled to touch it without reason. I couldn't help but think it would be such fun to put makeup on each of these sculpted faces.

The crowds pushed and punched and prodded me as they gushed by. I thought I'd better get inside. The doorknob, too, was a skull. No surprise. No one else was in the store. That was a surprise. The walls, ceiling, and floor were all made of the same wide-plank, dark wood. The knots in each plank, like eyes, watching me. It was freezing in there, so cold, I could see my breath. There was a scent I couldn't quite identify. Patchouli? Basil? Mildew? Densely packed, built-in book shelves lined the walls. The wooden floor creaked as I moved from shelf to shelf. Every book had a black binding and red cover. How organized it looked, so neat. Moving around the store, I scanned the bindings. No titles. Strange. Maybe this was a set for a photo shoot? For a performance? When I reached the end of one wall, I heard giggling. A quick look over my shoulder, but no one was there. The clock above the entry said six. The minute hand was moving, but apparently not doing its job. When I had grabbed my coffee at the hotel, it was almost ten. That couldn't have been more than fifteen minutes ago. Where was the proprietor? Why was no one else entering the store? I could see out the front window that the moving crowd was still rushing by like white-water rafters.

I felt a shadow, a presence as if someone were right behind me looking over my shoulder. Chills waltzed at the back of my neck. I debated whether to turn or not and decided to stretch my eyes left to see what I could see. Nothing. My overdeveloped imagination at play. A book to my right tilted forward. How gimmicky. In case someone was in hiding, watching me, I said aloud, "So, I'm supposed to open this book, and then what? Someone in costume is going to jump out from somewhere?" I reached for it and flipped through the pages. All blank. I opened another book. All blank. And another. The same. Bummer. Not a real bookstore. And no surprise scares. Is this a spooky funhouse-type room for tourists, and I'll be charged $20 when I leave? Maybe it's a venue for card readers, speakers, or some other evening event Salem offers during Haunted Happenings month to fill October. I looked around the room, top to bottom, wall to wall. Wonder what they'll be doing in here tonight? What's this set-up for? The intricate décor, the webs, carvings, etched glass, even the scent was proof someone went to quite a bit of trouble to create just the right look for this place. Too bad they can't make use of all this during the day. Seems like a waste. I heard giggling again.

I walked by every shelf. Took time to stare at the Hieronymous Bosch-type paintings on the walls, the wands and animal bones in shadowbox frames. I could taste the dust. In the far back corner, I noticed a wooden book case with a window-paned door filled with bottles, urns, and jars. Wow, the colors, the shapes. Had to take a closer look. They were works of art. If this were a store and there were a cash register, I'd buy one. They were that beautiful. Iridescent solids in jewel tones and swirled metallics webbing through deep, saturated, purple, sapphire, emerald. One on the lower shelf caught my eye. Is that real silver around the rim? It reminded me of a 1921 perfume bottle I have, green glass with art nouveau silver filigree. Some had lids with figural knobs on top. They were mesmerizing. I felt something, a tickle, like a feather, brush against my ear, and swiped at my face. Hoped it wasn't a spider. I hate spiders. I wanted out of there. I glanced at the clock. Two? Strange clock. It had said six just minutes ago. The clock seemed as confused as I was. Since I had left my hotel just before ten, I knew it could be neither six nor two. No way had I been in there more than twenty minutes. I reached for the doorknob and something reached for me. And giggled.

I jerked my leg, trying to get free. I tried to leave, but whatever it was tugged at my ankle pulling me back in. The giggling became louder. The cold was colder. The red books were shifting on their shelves ever so slightly, but I could hear the scratch of their cloth-covered bindings against the wood. I managed to pull the door open a small inch, but something or someone pushed the front door closed, and I had to pull my hand away to avoid losing a finger. The giggles stopped, and I heard a sing-song melody, and it wasn't pretty. I wanted to scream, "Go to hell," but thought whoever it was may already be there. I pulled at the door once more, it opened an inch or two, and slammed closed again. The singing stopped. The books settled. One more time, I pulled at the door with both hands. The door wouldn't budge. I dropped my arms to my side and stared at the skull-shaped doorknob. My body felt like it was made of oak. Scared stiff was no longer just a saying. I wanted to turn, to scan the room for the prankster, to find the hidden camera. I was as angry as I was scared. Could I trick it? Whatever it was. Or whoever. I stood cement-like. Don't know how long. No point looking up at the clock. I knew it would lie. I slowly lifted my hand to pull at the door again. It held solid. I heard the giggling. Then the singing again. "A Tisket, A Tasket?" "London Bridge Is Falling Down?" It had a childlike quality, but I couldn't pinpoint the melody. The giggling again. I spun around. The store was a still life. The books uniformly arranged as when I entered. Specs of dust, like a weightless ballet, moving through the ray of light slicing the storefront window. The sun's glint bouncing off the glass panes in the corner cabinet. I tried the doorknob again. I pulled hard, and the door flew open crashing against the wall.

I forced my way into the log-jam of Essex Street tourists. Rushing through the crowd, I collided with a man eating from a bag of caramelized peanuts. Unavoidable. "So sorry." On the street in the safety of the Indian-summer October sun and hundreds of people wearing coned hats and tee-shirts with trite sayings, like "Not Every Witch Lives in Salem," I turned to the bookstore front. I saw a face. Was that a little girl inside? I squinted. The longer I stood trying to focus, the more I was run off the cobble-stoned road by the families and teens anxious to reach a street performer just starting his act. I stood on my toes, peeked between bodies, stretched around strollers to stare toward the book store one more time, eyes fixed on the front window surrounded by skulls, and there she was behind the glass, her round face framed with auburn curls, dark circles beneath her eyes. She smiled at me. She had no teeth. And then I could tell she was laughing. She pointed at me, and I felt a grip on my ankle again. I jerked my leg and nearly kicked a passing beagle. When the toothless child in the store window stopped laughing, she waved to me. First, it was greeting-type wave, then it was an invitation. She wanted me to come back. I reached for the cross at the end of my neck chain. The little girl's smile shrunk to a vicious, hard line. She shook her head no, then she disappeared.

My cell buzzed. A text. "Where are you? It's 10. At the Bewitched statue." I forgot I had planned to meet Michael. Wait. Ten?

Maureen Mancini Amaturo is a New York based fashion and beauty writer and a contributing columnist for The Rye Record. She teaches Creative Writing, produces literary arts events for Manhattanville College, and leads the Sound Shore Writers Group, which she founded in 2007. Her personal essays and humor pieces have been published by Ovunque Siamo, Mothers Always Write, Bordighera Press, and Baseballbard.com. Her poetic tribute to John Lennon was published by the Beatlefest organization, and she's had articles and celebrity interviews published in local newspapers and on line.

ETCH ACROSS MY BONES
JONATHAN DOUGLAS DOWDLE

Write across my bones those words
That speak most to your being,
Gathering through the streets that are
Waiting for your eyes,
Gathering the world into the fever of your
Being, eyes sculpting as though breathing
The visions falling, the heart a vault
For secrets turned, stones that speak in
Memories, turned and held

Like a body waiting to settle into
Feeling; sensation beyond the dreaming,
Waking, from each thought as though it
Were only a prayer cast in a bottle,
Shattered in the shadows,
Opened by the first hand of
Light; a message toward the dawn
That the lips burned to answer.

Etch out through lines on skin, the map
That speaks in meaning, where touch is
Each emotion breathing, breath shared
That might come to confess;
The language that moves
Through the earth of you, digging into the ground
To take into the palms each fruit;

Taste the juice of meaning; revealing
How hunger is assuaged by its embrace.

Read through the book of vows you've written
As your spirit wakes from beneath the skin;
Speak your heart like rivers motion;
Flowing through each crack and crevice
To wash clean and feed the heart
Where the streets are named
Anew.

Keep these prayers in silent ways,
Where you might gather your face
Into your hands, the same as a child
Waiting for your touch to
Breathe it into life.

Gather from each heart your meaning,
Call it truth, or call it dreaming;
As the spirit settles into feeling;
Etch each word across my bones
That speak most to your being.

Jonathan Douglas Dowdle was born in Nashua, NH and has traveled throughout the US. He currently resides in South Carolina. Previous works have appeared or are appearing in: Blue Moon, Literary Heist, Peeking Cat Poetry, North Of Oxford, The Big Windows Review and various other magazines.

SUNRISE FROM UNTRACEABLE IMPROVISATIONS
JOSH HORNBERGER

For James

(adagio)

How did you know
the sensation of flight
just from watching the hawk?
It's happening, again
Must have been napping
Can you feel
the rise
of bones and feathers

(andante)

Those living skeletons,
humorous cartoons
of your youth
Imagination to a child
Spirits to a man
Finally,
off work. Were you too busy? Do you see the sunrise?

How did you know
how to channel someone else's energy
just from seeing them on tv?

(moderato)

Did you think that just because the venue closed down
that the light would cease?
But this energy reserve is crystalline and pure and indestructible
Highly ordered by divine fingerpaint
an appearance of glass but a substance unknowable

(allegro moderato)

Cheer up child your Father loves you, you're meant to be. Meeting
your hero is like going to universal studios theme park back to the
future and twister all so surreal or maybe like when you meet Big Bird
for the first time when you're 5 and haven't uncovered that it's just a
costume
What would it be like to have hundreds or thousands of people say
you changed my life or your art helped my soul
I praise God for sharing the cauldron, my turn to stir the cosmic stew
pot with ingredients like meatball galaxies and guitar string noodles
and potions.

(allegro)

And so now you know something about me and my friend that took
acid at a festival and couldn't speak if I'd have known the truth then
I'd have nicknamed him Zechariah (and when you get down to it god
isn't always pooh bear, jack) the tongue – tied father of john the
baptist but what if I told you you were blind too but didn't know it or
in a low solemn Morpheus voice that the simple word joy contains
mountains and kingdoms billions of exabytes of human data, saga all
great for a full feature film
Or billions of miles of instructions (which make computations of time

illusive) passed on by those who came before us that have already been born, bloomed, and died and are versed in the seasons. This road has been walked before, be still.

(mezzo – forte)

Personal hand written directions from sentient force, yes I mean Jehovah, you're real Father, the guy that lifts fire trucks.
It's true what they say he knows your name and if you thought all was going to be lost let me remind you that all things work for the good and maybe those skeletons didn't come from the closet but politely through the front door.

Josh Hornberger is an untrained yet optimistic poet from Indianapolis, IN. In addition to his love for writing, he is also proud to say that he has met 2 of the 4 members of the band Phish. Josh works in the food industry, and holds a seemingly arbitrary BA in International Relations. He has traveled to 3 continents outside of North America, is an avid music listener and coffee lover.

SHORT PIECES FOR THE XYLOPHONE (MINI-MEDITATIONS ON MORTALITY)
MICHAEL ZIMECKI

1. The sound of clanging bones

Europeans returning from the Crusades brought back finely crafted silks and other Arabian goods, games like chess, and an Arabic-Hindu numbering system that included the decimal point. They also brought back the very thing they had tried to export to the Holy Land: death on a massive and previously unknown scale. Following the trade routes that had opened up during the Crusades, the Black Death arrived on European shores in 1348. More than 50 million Europeans died before it ran its course.

Inspired by the Black Death, the Dance of Death or Danse Macabre became a common theme in the art, music and poetry of the late Middle Ages. Hans Holbein the Younger embroidered the theme in a series of 41 woodcuts published in 1538. The woodcuts featured the first known visual representation of an instrument, which like chess and the decimal point, was imported into Europe during the Crusades. The instrument, a xylophone, appears in two Holbein woodcuts from the Dance of Death series.

In the first of them (No. 25), a skeletal figure of Death plays a xylophone that appears to be made out of bones. He leads an old woman while a second figure of death takes her by the arm. A broken hourglass rests at her feet.

In the second (No. 33), a skeletal figure of Death leads an old man toward an open grave. An hourglass sits on a wall behind them. In the woodcut, Death carries a xylophone on a strap around his neck.

The xylophone is often associated with the sound of clanging bones. The French composer, Camille Saint-Saëns, was perhaps the first European to use the xylophone to that effect in his 1874 orchestral tone poem, Dans Macabre. In the piece, Death appears on Halloween and calls on his minions to rise from their graves and dance for him at the stroke of midnight. Henrik Ibsen subsequently used the piece in John Gabriel Borkman to forecast the death of his title character. Hedda Gabler plays it before she kills herself.

In 1929, Walt Disney made the dans macabre the subject of a cartoon short. In the Silly Symphony piece, Skeleton Dance, four skeletons hold hands and dance in a circle before one of them pulls the thigh bones off another and uses them to play the thigh less skeleton like a xylophone.

In the Simpsons' episode, The Itchy and Scratchy and Poochie Show, Homer is asked why Itchy produces two clearly distinct tones when he strikes the same rib in succession while playing Scratchy's skeleton like a xylophone in a prior episode. The question is somewhat rhetorical: neither Itchy nor Scratchy appears in the prior episode, production code 2F09, entitled Homer the Great.

Entropy is unidirectional. As Thomasina tells Septimus in Tom Stoppard's Arcadia, you can't stir the jam back out of the pudding. In the postmodern world, Holbein's woodcuts have been reduced to cartoons, but mortality is still with us.

2. The world's greatest xylophonist

His birth name was Abraham Himmelbrand and he learned his craft from Philip Rosenzweig, an immigrant who taught cimbalom in Warsaw and Paris before coming to America and devoting his life to the xylophone. The cimbalom, a musical sound box with metal or gut strings strung across one or two bridges, is played by striking the strings with a pair of metal mallets. Himmelbrand used hard mallets to strike the xylophone keyboard, using minimal efforts beyond the wrists, with almost no arm movement, much like a cimbalom player.

Born in New York on May 25, 1900, to Polish émigré parents, Himmelbrand played on the variety stage from the age of nine. He was discovered by Earl Fuller as a teenager and played in Fuller's Rector Novelty Orchestra as a xylophonist at Rector's Restaurant and other venues In New York City. An accomplished multi-instrumentalist, he also played piano at Healey's, a popular dining and dancing spot in midtown Manhattan noted for its beefsteak and wild nightlife.

After passage of the Volstead Act in October 1919, Himmelbrand got a gig playing the drums with Joseph C. Smith's dance band. He also played the xylophone for Smith on a Victor recording of "You're the One (That I Want)" that same year and on a Victor recording of "I lost my heart to you" in 1921.

In the early 1920s, Smith's band was featured at New York's Plaza Hotel, where Nick Carraway and Jordan Baker conversed in the tea garden in F. Scott Fitzgerald's The Great Gatsby. In 1924, Himmelbrand accompanied the band to Montreal and, the following year, to London.

Somewhere along the way, Himmelbrand adopted the stage name Teddy Brown. It was a wise career move. Anti-Semitism was on the rise. Automaker Henry Ford brought it onto the main stage of American life with publication of The International Jew, a work widely credited with influencing Adolph Hitler, who kept a photo of Ford on the wall of his Munich office, praised Ford in Mein Kampf, and later told a Detroit News reporter that Ford was his inspiration. As Ford's anti-Semitic gospel spread, universities reacted to "the Jewish problem" by imposing quotas on admission and tenure, employers by restricting job and promotion opportunities. Polish

Jews, like Teddy Brown's parents, were especially despised: scribes denounced them as "human parasites," accused them of bringing socialism to America, and exhorted politicians to prevent any more of them from immigrating to the United States. In response to these fears, Congress passed the Johnson-Reed Act in 1924, severely restricting immigration from Eastern Europe.

When the Joseph C. Smith band returned to the United States from England in the autumn of 1925, Teddy Brown stayed behind. Brown attributed his decision to the Duke of Windsor, whom, Brown claimed, had suggested he come to England. The decision was beneficial to Brown's career. He formed his own band, playing at the Café de Paris, where the Prince of Wales was a regular guest, and recording for the Imperial and Vocalion labels. He also toured the UK extensively, delighting audiences with his signature move: playing continuous scales on the xylophone while spinning around, an acrobatic feat for a man weighing 24 stone (336 pounds) or more.

In 1930, Teddy Brown appeared in Elstree Calling, a film co-directed by a young Alfred Hitchcock. Nominally the high point of Brown's career, the film role also was his lowest: at one point in the film, Brown cracks an anti-Semitic joke. "Have you ever seen a Hebrew parade?" he asks his band members before he bangs on a snare drum and quips, "To the bank, to the bank, to the bank, to the bank, to the bank."

Playing anti-Semitism for laughs may have helped Brown secure an audience in the England of the 1920s and 1930s. His sponsor, the Duke of Windsor, was an anti-Semite. In 1937, the Duke of Windsor and his new wife, the American divorcee Wallis Simpson, made an unofficial visit to Germany, where a beaming Adolph Hitler welcomed them. The visit came four years after the Duke was filmed encouraging the Queen Mother and a six-year-old Princess Elizabeth to give the Nazi salute, a rehearsal, perhaps, for the greeting he bestowed on Hitler during his 1937 visit.

A case also could be made that Brown's director, Hitchcock, shared the so-called 'drawing room" bigotry of the royals. In addition to Brown's anti-Semitic joke, Elstree Calling features a group of blackface dancers called "The Three Teddies," and Hitch's adaptation of Sean O'Casey's play, Juno and the Peacock, also released in 1930, included a stereotypical Jewish tailor with a large nose and an exaggerated eastern European accent, a character who is nowhere to be found in O'Casey's play.

After Elstree Calling, Brown devolved into self-parody. In the 1930s, he teamed with "The Crazy Gang," a group of British comedy entertainers. The enormously heavy Brown largely served as the butt of the Gang's jokes. He appeared with the Crazy Gang as a barman in the 1932 film Indiscretions of Eve and as "Slim Charlie" in the 1938 film Convict 99.

Teddy Brown's popularity peaked in the 1930s, although he did go on to share a stage with Glenn Miller at the Granada Cinema, Bedford, on November 26, 1944, a few weeks before the big band leader's aircraft disappeared in bad weather over the English Channel.

On April 29, 1946, Teddy Brown was billed as the World's Greatest Xylophonist in a new road show, "The Road to Laughter," opening at the Wolverhampton Hippodrome in Birmingham, England. Brown shared the bill with Alec Pleon, a yodeler and facial contortionist. Prior to his performance, Brown complained of a "twitch in his heart" and asked for a special room to be made up for him at the side of the stage so he could avoid climbing stairs to his dressing room. Once on stage, he needed to sit down for a spell. He died shortly after 5 the following morning. The Birmingham coroner ruled the death a coronary thrombosis, and Brown's body was cremated at Golden Green Crematorium in London. His ashes were returned to America by his widow, Sophie, and are interred in Mount Hebron Cemetery, Flushing, Queens County, New York under the name, Abraham "Teddy Brown" Himmelbrand.

3. Sic transit inglorius mundi

"Sic transit gloria mundi,"
"How doth the busy bee,"
"Dum vivimus vivamus,"
I stay mine enemy!
— Emily Dickinson

"You could be ignorant and be a star. You could be a moron and be wealthy," comedian Fred Allen said of vaudeville, the most popular form of American entertainment from its rise in the 1880s to its demise in the 1930s. "Vaudeville asked only that you owned an animal or an instrument, or have a minimum of talent and a maximum of nerve."

The xylophone was the instrument of choice for many vaudevillians. Dave Monahan played one – with his hands and feet. Monahan, a self-proclaimed "wizard of the xylophone," would mount a high stool in back of his xylophone to tap a tune with his feet while holding two long-handled mallets in each hand. Variety-star Will Mahoney went Monahan one better by attaching mallets to his feet and playing his xylophone by standing on it. Mahoney, best known for a tap-dancing routine that quite literally incorporated pratfalls, specially modified his xylophone so he could dance upon it, prompting Fred Allen to observe that if Mahoney had spent the same amount of thinking as he did on his xylophone, he might have discovered penicillin. Mahoney's specially adapted instrument was purchased by Elton John from Mahoney's widow after the vaudeville performer's death.

Late in his career, Dave Monahan adapted Fred Allen's suggestion that a vaudeville act required an instrument or an animal, by incorporating animals, –sort of–in his xylophone act. Monahan added his "amazing madcap monkeys and portly musical puppets" to his foot-playing skills, having his puppets play the xylophone alongside him.

The son of Irish Catholic immigrants, Fred Allen, born John Florence Sullivan, had adopted a succession of stage names, including Freddy James and Benjamin Franklin, before settling on the one that made him famous, taken from Revolutionary War hero, Ethan Allen. Like Fred Allen, many other vaudevillians and variety stars changed their names to hide their ethnicity. The Jewish xylophonist Abraham Himmelbrand, for example, adopted the stage name Teddy Brown. Xylophonist Basil Garwood Lambert took another tack, sticking a vowel on the end of his surname to make it sound foreign and exotic.

Billing himself as "the world's daffiest xylophonist," Valparaiso, Indiana-born Lambert adopted the stage name, Professor Lamberti, and transformed a mishap on the vaudeville stage into career-changing shtick. The mishap occurred when a magician's duck escaped and wandered on the stage behind Lamberti while he was playing his xylophone. The crowd went wild. Lamberti exchanged the magician's duck for a stripper, who would disrobe behind him, while he continued to play on his xylophone. Dressed in zany clothes and acting indifferent to the stripper's performance while the audience ramped up its applause, Lamberti always ended his set by chasing the woman off stage with a seltzer bottle. Lamberti, who appeared onstage with Phil Silvers, the Three Stooges, and Rita Hayworth, among others, during the course of his long career, once said that you couldn't make a living with the xylophone "if you played it right."

Xylophone pioneer and composer George Hamilton Green was one musician who tried to play the instrument, not just correctly, but beautifully. Green's compositions, recorded by Disney and others, inspired a whole generation of percussionists, including jazz great Red Norvo, who taught himself how to play the vibraphone by listening to Green's xylophone solos. Green entered vaudeville at the age of 19 but later strove to elevate the status of the xylophone by making it a part of the modern orchestra. Sadly, he watched his career dwindle from his zenith as a star soloist in the 1920s to a studio sideman a couple of decades later. One day in November 1946, Green stopped playing during a live radio broadcast, set down his mallets, and walked out of the studio, never to play again. He started a second career as a cartoonist.

Vaudeville, as Fred Allen observed and Green eventually recognized, valued novelty over art. The curtain came down on the variety stage a long, long time ago, but, even today, one can still become a star with a minimum of talent and a maximum of nerve. "Imitation," Fred Allen said of one of the media that succeeded vaudeville, "is the sincerest form of television," a "medium" where "anything well done is rare." Allen was suspicious of "furniture that talked," his description for TV, and he held Hollywood in even lower regard. "You can take all the sincerity in Hollywood," Allen once said, "place it in the navel of a fruit fly and still have room for three caraway seeds and a producer's heart."

Sic transit, vaudeville; sic transit, Harvey Weinstein; it all passes. Or, to paraphrase Emily Dickinson, dum vivimus bibamus–while we live, let's drink.

Michael Zimecki is the author of a novel, Death Sentences. His nonfiction work has appeared in The National Law Journal, Harper's Magazine, and College English, among other publications. He lives in Pittsburgh, Pennsylvania with his wife, Susan.

FLESHING IT OUT
THERESA BAKER

When I write
a lightbulb goes off in the skull, the idea forming.
What do I want to say?
free verse or form
then I keep adding bones to the skeleton.
Where the rhymes are
the line breaks, the ending
how they feel when their eyes touch the last word.
Then the organs and flesh to complete it.
what words make you laugh, cry, or puke
capitals and punctuation that would make an English teacher blush.
And when a poem is fully formed, will readers accept Frankenstein's
new monster?

Theresa Baker has been both reading and writing poetry since elementary school, and won a contest in fifth grade. She looked into publishing in 2018, and this is her first publication. She currently lives in Indianapolis with a job at her dream zoo.

LA NOVICIA VOLANDO
ANITA CABRERA

La Novicia Volando touched down
on a skinny stretch of hot Chilean beach
south of the bus station
where old women smelling of tea and grief
peddle black oyster ceviche
at 9:00 a.m.
and men whisper bargains
on tarantulas
as big as a brother's hand
crucified on balsa wood
furry striped-kneed spider legs akimbo
for someone else's sins.

The Flying Nun alit
amidst scattered sea lion bones
to rest
without the weight of a habit
and warm herself on the rocks
that jut into the ocean
altars
for the washed up leftovers
of sea creatures so common
they're forgotten.

La Novicia Volando landed–
a miracle
(milagro de milagros)

to a horny sixteen-year old local
who had never met
a nun
in such a small a bikini bottom
and teeth that white
who could sing
the songs of Vincente Fernandez
in a Yankee accent
grind groins
against the sunning boulders
with the stripped remains
of ordinary mammals.

Later, nobody would believe
that the Flying Nun touched down on him.

Anita Cabrera's short fiction, poetry and creative nonfiction explore the themes of addiction, mental illness and the complex nuances in parent-child relationships and marriage. Her work has appeared in The Berkeley Fiction Review, The Berkeley Poetry Review, Brain, Child Magazine, Colere, Acentos, MomEgg Review, The Ravensperch, Deronda Review and the Squaw Valley Poetry Review. Ms. Cabrera lives in San Francisco, CA where she teaches, dances, and rides bikes, but not necessarily in that order.

THE ACCIDENTAL BONEYARD
KY J. DIO

There is a place about 29 miles outside of town (it is not actually mine!). Does not belong to me. There is no street sign, real estate, or property value listed anywhere. At least not that I can find. I am not sure who actually owns it. Some people camp there, sometimes.

I like to think that it is a forgotten place. Only twice have I seen traces and tracks of other humyns there. There are many gravel roads and cattle guards to meet before you will arrive. There is no secret treasure map of how to get there. You cannot drop a pin.

From what I can tell, it used to be a shooting range of some sort. I'm sure the Forest Service called it something, once. The only barrier to this destination is knowing its location. A simple turn off along a long, long road to somewhere else with a metal gate and a sign that says You Are Welcome. Make sure to close me behind you. Sometimes there are traffic cones and smiley faces and stickers to meet you at the gate.

It is a purely magical place. A loop around turn off on the side of a mountain a few miles past what these Arizona people call a lake. My bones were bathed in Minnesota lake bed wet clay sand.

So I can tell you this is no lake.

But I always close the gate behind me and leave no trace. Mostly I pick up trash and really, really, I come here to find bones. I'm no scientist, but I am an artist, and I hope that that means something most days.

There's something that bears no name who keeps drawing me back to the accidental boneyard. In the pines, among the tree line, amid the whistles that come from mouths of sediment layered teeth - there is something out there that calls it's marrow to meet mine.

213

And I always find the bones. As soon as you enter the deep canyon forest wall of wilderness, loop around to the rock face plateau, there is relief among the quiet – every step sounding an explosion to the forest floor. Every breath a time bomb. Every bone a prize.

There are three main spots that open up to little campground areas with burned-out fireplaces -gravel everything and bumper to bumper peak lines that coat the pine trees, leaves, and mangled trees that sleep beneath. Here and there, baby cactus who will always bite you if you tread too lightly.

Among the forest floor, nestled in the barks and the shells and the gravel and the ghosts – are bones. Hip bones. Leg bones. Joints and sinew. All parts and parcels of animals I cannot name. Maybe do not want to. I pick them up carefully to make sure I am keeping the ones I collect together, making sure to look around to see what other marrows I can find. It is my favorite treasure hunt and from what I can tell I hope I am one of the only ones to come across this accidental moonlit graveyard of bones.

The last time I took my lover. The fourth time so much smoke was blowing in from the south that we were choking on the sunset. Breathing it all in. He was the one who noticed the shells, gave place and meaning to the weather vanes, trails of broken glass and shotgun shells, bent practice magazines and metal targets. I had just assumed it was a parcel that had just seen a lot of parties. But he showed me differently.

It was the only time I had taken someone else out there. It was the time I found the most bones and I took them all home. To boil them, Clean them, and make them into something beautiful again. Breathing life back into death and rot. Repurposing death into art. I would like to think these animals I cannot name died peacefully. Were eaten or carried off by coyote. Or vermin. That the circle of life was completed and that I came to find them. Took them home. Cleaned them. Honored them. Blessed them. And swallowed Mother Earth's reason to honor the dead. And find myself among the gravel, treading so carefully, searching the forest floor for the things that were never meant to be buried.

Ky J. Dio is a host and Administrator for Juniper House Readings, a Slam Poet, a facilitator of creative writing workshops, and the author of 5 chapbooks. She makes recycled acrylic and spray paint art, and works as a Jewelry Specialist at a pawn shop. She lives in Flagstaff, Arizona.

S.E.L.
SARAH NICHOL STRUNK

My body burns for you
Like hell awaiting its sinners
Take me into your searing embrace
Keep me there for all eternity
Do with me what you will
Rip the flesh from my bones
To reveal what's within
Tear the muscle, fiber by fiber
Unravel my existence
Feed on my flesh, drink my blood
Engulf me, let me flow through you
Let me make your heart race
Let me make your blood rise
Let me coarse through your veins
The very essence which is you
Feel me inside of you
Like I do with every living breath
Feed into me by feeding on me
Until there is nothing left
Until you've engulfed me
By picking my bones clean

Sarah Nichol Strunk grew up as a military brat and has currently settled in Cleveland, Ohio. She uses her art as a way to communicate to the world in ways she cannot verbally or in person. She views the world as weird and whimsical which she tries to convey through her art.

Y / BAD MAN / BAD MAN 2
MARC CARVER

Y

I walk out in the street and people smile at me
and wave at me
what the hell do they do it for
I really don/t know but still they do it
like I am some champion
I just made it out of the house
and that is a big thing for me
maybe they see it
look he made it out of the house today
good for him
but they all look
like they are astonished
here he is
thank you
because without you
I would have nothing

BAD MAN

You have to be a bad man
to be a poet
you have to be disturbed

you don't even have to know why
but know that is why you can
and if you ever find out
it doesn't really help you
or make you a better poet
if anything it may make you worse
but now you know
why you started
and if you want
you can stop

BAD MAN 2

I am not a great man
I am weak
I am not too clever
I am all sorts of bad
I am not even a good writer
Even when people tell me I am
I DON'T BELIEVE THEM.
I like to tell the truth
but people really don't want that
but still I give it to them
I drink
I drink
I push people away before they hurt me
I hurt them.
Now people don't want to know me at all
and to be honest
I don't blame them

Marc Carver has published ten collections of poetry but to him the most important thing is to get an email from someone he does not know that says they enjoy his work.

LOSING CONTROL
JOSEPH HIGDON

The first cancer-eaten bone that broke
caused my mother to collapse at the doorstep
and scrape her face against the gravel driveway.

The second rotted bone that broke
loosened her from my ignorant grip,
and she scraped her face again
against the grit and gravel.

The frail bones that forced her
into the hospital soon confined her
to this medical bed at home.

As she lay
facing her last hours,
I asked
if losing control
frustrated her the most.

Tears pooled in her pale eyes,
and a faint nod
sent them spilling
over the surface wound scabs.

I told her how a young boy on a bike
once roared "Vroooom"
past my house down the road,

then returned and wheelied,
returned again, "Swoosh—swoosh"
as he slalomed the pot holes,
then swerved in and out of the ditch,
"Heeeeen—yah!" with each switch
of his imaginary gears.

When I explained the impression it left
that we work all our lives
to gain independence
and practice self-control,
then dread surrendering
in the end,

my mother's clammy hand crawled to mine;
her feeble fingers clung once,
weakened and lay lifeless—
our last exchange
before she let go of this world.

Joseph Higdon has an Associates degree from Kellogg Community College, a Bachelor of Arts in English education from Western Michigan University and a journalism minor from Michigan State University. A former high school English and journalism teacher, he now works in production with the goal of becoming a training and development specialist. He has had poems and short stories published in small college journals, local newspapers and library anthologies.

BONES / LONGING
SUZANNE BURNS

BONES

Remember the December afternoon
my bones spoke to your bones?
Beneath my lace shirt, my clavicle
just waiting to be noticed, its
close-up collared around my neck
as it strained towards that one
spectacular blue shirt. A shirt
even Daisy Buchanan would notice
with her West Egg voice full of money.
Your bones brushing against my bones
makes me rich in a way that feels
stronger than Jay Gatsby's diamonds.
Who needs a narrator when our bones
translate the longing of skin into structure?
In that one embrace my thoracic curve
danced towards yours better than a waltz
in any old movie. Of course my heart gallops
beneath my bones when your blue shirt nears,
but what about the others? Twelve hearts sit
inside my spine and inside your spine, our
vertebrae faceted together in bony gossip
as they conspire to break each other open
and see the hard love tokens inside,
for skeletons yearn without permission.
If you could only see the way yours

walks towards me before your heart
or mind have a chance to catch up.
If you could only see the way mine arranges
each outfit into the fashion of flesh waiting
for your bones to undress. My locked
jaw, my clicking of ribs, how they realign
to accept your ribs, the brutal crush of symmetry,
the ease of a perfect fit.

LONGING

1.
I have you in the way
of not having you.
This means we will never fight
over how to cut a tomato
or how to make a bed,

though you could douse
a mattress in gasoline
and throw the match my way if,
before the burning,
I got one chance to have you
beyond not having you.

2.
Your newfound muscles are a way
of touching without having you,
a game of hide and seek,
the growing hardness beneath,

though I would linger just as long
if you had no muscles,
if you were soft,
if you were only bones.

If those bones, someday, took up
residence in a science class
I would break in at night
to waltz you around the room

until Love asked me to, please,
love you a little less,
this skeleton who still loves being loved.

3.
The last time I saw you,
your left hand became a deity,
the veins beneath branched,
beatific tributaries,
the Stations of the Cross
of a religion you don't belong to
and I've forgotten to follow,

the blood beneath your skin
holy because it's kept you
standing this long.

If I had you, then,
I would have touched your hand,
almost smelling of the future
burnings between us,
but felt grateful you did not
belong to me because,

if I touched your hand the way
I've always wanted to touch your hand,
I would never be able to figure out
how to let go.

Suzanne writes both poetry and prose in central Oregon. She is currently working on a new novel in between competitive baking at local county fairs.

MUSIC STILLBORN, OR JUST INTERRUPTED
HOLLY DAY

Strewn with the bones of sailors lured to its rocky shores
By sirens singing songs of love and sometimes loneliness
Arms outstretched to passing ships as if in joyous embrace.
A broken heart floats on a cold, neurotic sea.

The waters beat upon the beach in bone-crushing white embrace
Death himself parks his ferry sometimes close to shore
A cold wind blowing at his back, bearing his loneliness.
The coastline ringed by monsters guarding the deep, neurotic sea

On the decks of passing ships, sailors stuff their ears against the
loneliness
Aim their ships at the dark horizon, away from gloomy shores
and mermaid songs on rocky cliffs and whispered dreams, the cold
embrace
of roaring waves glittering high above the cold, neurotic sea.

Holly Day's poetry has recently appeared in Plainsongs, The Long Islander, and The Nashwaak Review. Her newest poetry collections are In This Place, She Is Her Own (Vegetarian Alcoholic Press), A Wall to Protect Your Eyes (Pski's Porch Publishing), Folios of Dried Flowers and Pressed Birds (Cyberwit.net), Where We Went Wrong (Clare Songbirds Publishing), and Into the Cracks (Golden Antelope Press).

ENDINGS
NATE RAGOLIA

When I started BONED five years ago, it was a simple, silly idea. "What if we just wrote stories with bones and skeletons in them?" Now, 285 stories, poems, essays, plays, a comic, and some original art later, it's clear to me that this little experiment was more than just an excuse to write, but a conversation between writers and readers about the essence of life.

Our bones hold us up, they contain our organs, they allow our motility. They represent our capacity for courage... for we're only spineless when we're cowardly. They make us solid and whole. And that's what the writing here has done for me. To have spent the last five years collecting, editing, and sharing this immense haul of incredible work was a true blessing. And that makes it emotional to say goodbye, but it is time.

I had wanted to write some fiction for this last post, something final and comprehensive to punctuate everything that BONED has been, but it would do a disservice to act as if there's a story-based ending to such an amazing collaboration as this one. BONED isn't about me, or my writing. It's about each of us who contributed. I have made incredible friends, many of whom I now talk with regularly, because of this project. I have been elated to read works that made me jealous of their talented scribes. I have been brought to laughter and to tears and felt hope and fear and joy... all because of the writers who trusted BONED to share their words.

The beauty of the internet, despite all of its incredible and disturbing misuses and abuses, is that the words here will exist in perpetuity (barring the sudden collapse of WordPress... or society, of course). BONED will forever be a time capsule of this project, of its writers, of some of my own work, and the work of friends who have since passed from this world. Perhaps that's a little too florid, but I like to think of it as important because it was important to me, and it was an honor to share all the excellent writing we have published.

So, thank you. Thank you! THANK YOU! If you're here, you've read some of this work, making a writer's life better (and believe me, being read *does* make a writer's life better), or you've contributed, making my life better... or maybe you stumbled upon this by accident, in which case I ask you to take some time to read the work here, to feel the feels, to embrace the bones inside us all that make us equal, fragile, resilient, and meaningful.

Be well and stay safe,

Nate

BONED: A Collection of Skeletal Writings is a project started by Nate Ragolia in 2016. Each Tuesday, a new story, poem, play, or essay posts. The common theme is that all content features either bones, or a skeleton, in some capacity. BONED hung up its skeleton at the end of 2020.

Read the archives at bonedstories.wordpress.com,

ABOUT THE PUBLISHING TEAM

Nate Ragolia was labeled "weird" early in school, and it stuck. He's a lifelong lover of science fiction, and a nerd/geek. In 2015 his first book, *There You Feel Free,* was published by 1888's Black Hill Press. He's also the author of *The Retroactivist*, published by Spaceboy Books. He founded and edits BONED, an online literary magazine, has created webcomics, and writes whenever he's not playing video games or petting dogs.

Shaunn Grulkowski has been compared to Warren Ellis and Phillip K. Dick and was once described as what a baby conceived by Kurt Vonnegut and Margaret Atwood would turn out to be. He's at least the fifth best Slavic-Latino-American sci-fi writer in the Baltimore metro area. He's the author of *Retcontinuum,* and the editor of *A Stalled Ox* and *The Goldfish,* all for 1888/Black Hill Press.

Antoine Valot, Graphics Bot is a 2015 Nexus™ series Replicant from the Tyrell Corporation, communications/design model. He enjoys designing book covers, nitpicking about words, functioning within his operating margins, and making the most of the two years he has left to live.

Learn more about Spaceboy Books at readspaceboy.com

This book features the font Skullphabet by Noah Scalin (Skull-A-Day). Learn more about Skull-A-Day at skulladay.blogspot.com

www.ingramcontent.com/pod-product-compliance
Lightning Source LLC
Chambersburg PA
CBHW020105180626
46812CB00006B/2472